# LIES, LIES, MORE LIES

## How to Create and Build Fictional Characters

Taught by Jules Swales

**BASED ON JACK GRAPES' METHOD WRITING CONCEPTS**

Published in Partnership with

IW Press

Lies, Lies and More Lies
Copyright © 2024 by Jules Swales
First Published in Great Britain in partnership with IW Press Ltd

All rights reserved. No part of this book may be reproduced in any form or by any means without permission in writing from the author, except for inclusion of brief quotations in a review.

Cover image created by Iain Hill of 1981D
Cover design by 1981D
Interior design by Chapter One Book Design

A catalogue record of this book is available from the British Library.

ISBN-13: 978-1-916701-09-0 (Paperback)
ISBN-13: 978-1-916701-10-6 (e-book)

IW Press Ltd, 62-64 Market Street, Ashby-de-la-Zouch, England, LE65 1AN
https://www.iliffe-wood.co.uk/

## LIST OF AUTHORS

JULES SWALES

BIANCA BAZIN
TSILAH BURMAN
KRYSTEEN DVORACEK
MARGO GEORGE
FIONA JACOB
CHRISTINE MANDER
TRISH POMEROY
HILDA RHODES
MARY WHITE

(MARIA ILIFFE-WOOD)
(JB HOLLOWS)

# PRAISE FOR *LIES, LIES AND MORE LIES*

*Lies, Lies and More Lies* is a marvellous collection of lively, compelling fictional character portraits. But it's much more than that. It gave me a process that opened new vistas of creativity and poetic freedom for my future work!
— Steve Chandler, International and Bestselling Author of *Shift Your Mind Shift the World*

Storytelling is the ultimate craft. *Lies, Lies and More Lies* is filled with multiple exercises to help you develop your craft while being entertained by the artistry of emerging voices in the field.
— Michael Neill, Bestselling Author of *Creating the Impossible* and *The Inside-Out Revolution*

The idea that lying makes you a more creative writer was news to me! I love how this book is laid out with step-by-step instructions based on the writing concept. Then, writing samples from her students are shared, based on those concepts.
— Tricia Nelson, Internationally Acclaimed Author, Transformational TEDx Speaker and Emotional Eating Expert, Founder of Heal Your Hunger

This collection was totally captivating. These are mini, espresso-sized shots of intrigue and mystery. The glorious introduction of each briefing allowed me to see the constraint, get it intellectually, and then dive into the stories and marvel at them.
— Lorna Davis, Former CEO, Personal Coach

*Lies, Lies and More Lies* is packed with exercises and tips for writers to help access their deep voice, their "personal molten interior," and create complex, believable characters so real, they jump off the page.
— Alexis Rhone Fancher, Method Writer, Author of ten collections, including *BRAZEN, The Dead Kid Poems, EROTIC: New & Selected*, and *Triggered*

You are first treated to the exercises authors are invited to undertake, you then get to enjoy the interpretation, and then you get the gift of engaging with what is written. The beauty lies in the variety and willingness of the authors to be vulnerable in their response to the questions. A thoroughly enjoyable read!

— Dr Jen Frahm, Global Expert in Change and Organisational Transformation. Keynote Speaker, Entrepreneur, Author of *Conversations of Change*, *The Agile Change Playbook* (with Lena Ross), and *Change. Leader: The changes you need to make first*

*Lies, Lies and More Lies* is a wild ride of a book. I found myself wanting to spend more time with the person I had just met on the page! I was blown away at the colorful variety of each character.

— Jamie Fiore Higgins, Financial Times 25 Most Influential Women, Author of *Bully Market*

Gripped throughout the whole read. This was visceral. This story upset me, held me and intrigued me. Those terrors which people live through, in the context of their lives, yet inexplicably relatable, brought to the fore—a reader seriously moved.

— Charlie Hall, Fashion Model

This book is a beautifully written reflection of the nature of our humanity. The highs, lows, victories and pains, all wrapped up in short snappy writings that are a joy to read.

— Julianne Del Cano-Kennard. Author, Wholality® Originator, NDE Experiencer and International Speaker

I feel intrigued, provoked, and saddened by the characters I met in this book. I guess that means they all succeeded. The reader encounters an array of characters, language, perceptions, and offences that prompt a reaction.

— Matt Goddard, Creator of the WORK Principle, Spiralling Upwards, and the Courageous Leaders Forum

What an amazing process to build character and how creatively the students have drawn on their own deeper shadows and aspects of themselves into the brief tantalizing narratives. I was drawn into the stories wanting each one to continue.

— Karen Foy MSc, ICF Master Certified Coach, Coach Supervisor, and Mentor. Honorary Fellow, University of Reading

This book made so much sense to me, especially the use of Stanislavski's tools. Having the writers begin with character to develop everything else in good storytelling was brilliant. The writer's works were completely transformed from truth to lies.

— Doreen Calderon, Hollywood Actor and Coach

I found the assignment fascinating. I couldn't help but try to guess what was true and what was a lie. I appreciate the authors embracing the assignment. It made for an interesting—and fun—read.

— Janice Minsberg, Emmy-nominated Producer

I love how the writers use the artistry of words in different ways to create compelling stories and characters. I find it gratifying to see how we can use memory to not just relive past events but to tell stories that are in service to others.

— Mavis Karn MA, LSW, Author of *It's That Simple, A User's Guide for Human Beings*

This book is a sense-twanging collage of the most evocative, raw and humorous, short writings from some talented writers. I love the diversity of how it was written and the uniqueness of each imaginative story. In essence, bloody fantastic!

— Rudiger Kennard. Author, Wholality® Originator, International Speaker, and Award-winning Filmmaker

A series of eye-opening insights into the art of writing fiction from the deepest, truest voice of the writer. It is fascinating how the teacher describes the art of storytelling and character development. The excellent writing of the authors is spellbinding.

— Clare Dimond, Author of *REAL*

A challenging read, an emotional roller coaster with the stories' progression revealing a sense of deep loss, betrayal of trust, unmet expectations and anger with many mental cliff edges to fall over, recover from before moving on to the next story.

— David Finlayson BSc, MSc, DIC, Lay Member of Court (the Board), Glasgow University, Former Deputy Chairman Brunel University, London

I loved being exposed to the dark secrets causing the twists and turns in each piece and how as writers we unwittingly find ourselves in our fictional characters.

— Amanda L. Mottorn, Author of *Finding Moksha: One Woman's Path in Uncertain Times and Artist*, American Abstract Expressionist Painter of Nature, City & Sea Scenes

Reading *Lies, Lies and More Lies* was inspirational and intriguing. Using lies as a tool in character development was fascinating. It made me want to do the exercises. The essays were rich in depth and character development. I was entertained and moved.

— Pat Heys, Retired Nurse, Personal Development Coach

I can sniff out dud character creation in a book, so how hard could it be to create one myself? Answer: very. By the end of Part 1 I had developed a deep admiration for the participants, which only grew with each exercise.

— Jess Macdermot, Global Director, Media Company

The authors write in a way that is unapologetic and does not waver—characters come through in a clear and authentic way. Many of these pieces had a little twist or zinger in the last line. As a writer, a method that allows for lying is intriguing to me.

— Sheila Path-McMahon, Author, High School English Teacher, Co-Regional Advisor of the Illinois Chapter of the Society for Children's Book Writers and Illustrators

I love the concept, the layout, the way Jules skillfully sets up each section of the book. Then we are treated to well written, intriguing pieces from the authors. I find myself inspired and curious and really want to go on a 'Character Date'!

— Lara Lauder, Regional Director, The Athena Network: West Berks Creating Connections | Inspiring Success

This is a fascinating mix of creative writing exercises and short stories. It provides a unique insight into the creative writing process. The short stories are varied both in tone and approach. Their range and vibrancy demonstrate the value of the course.

— Dr David Huxley, Editor in Chief, Journal of Graphic Novels and Comics

Wicked good reading! *Lies, Lies and More Lies* is a testament to the human imagination and the delicious interplay between fact and fiction in every human character. The writing will keep you guessing, laughing, awash in empathy and disgusted in turn!

— Linda Sandel Pettit, Ed.D. Visionary Guide, Author, Speaker, Podcaster and Blogger, Author of *Leaning into Curves: Trusting the Wild Intuitive Way of Love*

*For all those authors who think
they can't write great characters.
You can.
And here's how.*

# CONTENTS

Foreword ... i
Introduction to *Lies, Lies and More Lies* ... iii
A Little About Jack Grapes ... vii

**PART 1**

20% Lies—And Why We Do It ... 1
A Time To Live, A Time To Die ... 5
The Best Pie Ever ... 7
Odd Duck ... 9
The Homecoming ... 11
I Longed For A Past That Didn't Exist ... 13
Lucky To Be Alive ... 15
A Child's Despair ... 17
In My Head ... 19
Not Boring ... 21

**PART 2**

50% Lies ... 25
It's No Surprise I'm Single ... 27
Strange Characters ... 29
Broken Widow ... 31
Pigs Might Fly ... 33
Staccato Dancer ... 35
The Accused ... 37
Half-Read Books ... 39
Death Of A Dream ... 41
I Wish He'd Called Me A Cunt ... 43

**PART 3**

| | |
|---|---|
| Jack Grapes' Character Template©—Character Date | 47 |
| No Beef | 50 |
| Kookaburra Swoops | 54 |
| Stranger to Her Heart | 58 |
| Scars | 62 |
| Ring Finger | 66 |
| The Designer | 70 |
| Death by Oleander | 74 |
| Make Lemonade When Life Gives You Lemons | 78 |
| Fascism Never Sleeps | 82 |

**PART 4**

| | |
|---|---|
| 75% LIES | 89 |
| Culchie | 91 |
| Allie and Me | 93 |
| I'll Hunt Them Down | 95 |
| An Open Window | 97 |
| Mother Knows Best | 99 |
| Luckiest, Happiest People in the World | 101 |
| Inheritance | 103 |
| Buttercups | 105 |
| Today is a Good Day to Die | 107 |

**PART 5**

| | |
|---|---|
| Unreliable Narrator | 111 |
| Devout | 114 |
| Mercy, Mercy Me | 116 |
| My Last Day at the Bank | 118 |
| Hide and Seek | 120 |
| Stepping Over Christmas | 122 |
| An Unexpected Life | 124 |

| | |
|---|---|
| Cedar-wood Doors | 126 |
| The Shovel | 128 |
| The Perfect Baby | 130 |
| | |
| Addendum by Jack Grapes | 133 |
| Connect With Us | 139 |
| What To Read Next | 141 |
| Acknowledgements | 142 |
| A Note About Royalties | 144 |
| About Jules Swales | 145 |
| About Our Authors | 146 |
| About Maria Iliffe-Wood | 151 |
| About JB Hollows | 152 |
| Bibliography | 153 |

# FOREWORD

I've been privileged to be a student of Jules Swales from the very first pilot program many years ago, when she first started teaching Jack Grapes' Method Writing. The Character Class session, based on "Creating and Building a Fictional Character," from Jack Grapes' "Flip Side-B" Method Writing Program has to be, hands down, one of my favourites. It was the most fun class to attend, once I got over the idea of telling lies on the page. It's pretty common for students to be uncomfortable with lying. I liked to think of myself as being an honest bod. But once I got the hang of it, there was no turning back.

Each week the students were invited to sprinkle their writing, to varying degrees, with lies. The result? Surprising, interesting and deep characters. It's stunning to me the breadth and depth of characters that show up.

None of the writers in this book have a fiction writing background. They have been studying with Jules Swales for two years plus and I think they would all agree that when they began classes, they would not have been able to produce such wonderful characters. They all started with Level 1/The Basics; Writing Like You Talk, Transformation Line, Image Moment and Dreaded Association, together with the Level Two voices, all exercises that come from Jack Grapes' books;

*Method Writing—The First Four Concepts,* and *Advanced Method Writing—The Art of Tonal Dynamics.*

The most fun was going on the Character Date. Out to a local cafe, spotting some unsuspecting person and making up a whole backstory about them. Then using this fictitious information to write about the character, either in third person or first person. You'll see some brilliant examples of both the Character Template and the stories that emerged.

This book is divided up into sections, each correlates with a week of the class. At the beginning of each part, you'll find suggestions about how to approach the exercise, followed by examples from her students. One thing to remember is that nobody started with a character in mind. The character emerged as the student focused on the exercise.

The authors in this book hail from all parts of the world: the UK, USA, Australia, Ireland, and Sweden, so you will find a mix of American and English vocabulary. You'll also find language that is as colourful as the characters.

I hope you give the exercises a go. The best way would be to read one part at a time, and then follow the instructions and write your own character piece. Then move on to the next part. If you like, go on a Character Date.

Have fun and do let us know how you get on.

*Maria Iliffe-Wood*

# INTRODUCTION TO LIES, LIES AND MORE LIES

## Write Great Fictional Characters

All the exercises in this book, plus the Character Template, are based on "Creating and Building a Fictional Character," from Jack Grapes' "Flip Side-B" Method Writing Program, itself based on Stanislavski's book *Building a Character*.

A thank you to the writers who contributed to this book. It is no small feat to step out from behind the safety of "at-home sofa writing," and share your work with the world. The writers in this compilation series did just that. And a big thank you to Jack for creating these amazing exercises.

Let's jump in. There are myriad online forums, blogs, posts, and master classes on the art of writing good character, and it's hard. Writers try the "come up" with a good plot/story idea, and then hope the characters will emerge. Another train of thought is to find characters by creating lists about them, sort of like mood boards, to flush them out. I found this tricky. The "back-to-front" vagueness of my characters made them "out there" somewhere, and it was my job to try and lasso them onto the page and into story. Without a doubt, Jack's exercises in the

Character Class offered me the best way to develop rich and interesting characters.

Yes, of course, honing in on the details of characters is imperative, and fun to do. You will read more about this in chapter three. The key to a rich character is their depth, their conscious and unconscious desires, and their complexities.

> *I understood, through rehab, things about creating characters. I understood that creating whole people means knowing where we come from, how we can make a mistake, and how we overcome things to make ourselves stronger.*
> — Samuel L. Jackson

I learned many years ago, in my classes with Jack, that good character comes first and foremost from me. From my life, my conscious and unconscious desires, my complexities (I have many) my loves, and my flaws (I have many). These things, married with the unique and true voice of the writer, me—the voice many never seem to grasp—are what provide the creative vortex necessary from which awesome characters are born.

It's not the surface reporting voice I'm referring to. Gritty, complicated, interesting characters come from the writer's "deep voice." What sets Jack's program apart from so many others is that the exercises invite the writer to discover their own deep voice, their personal molten interior. Without that skill, it becomes very difficult to write good characters.

Think of it this way, as explained by Jack Grapes: the writer's authentic *voice creates the character, character creates the plot, plot creates the story*. Horse first, cart behind, writer at the reins.

> *But when creating a fictional narrator, it's important for the writer—not just to develop fictional facts and feelings—but the narrator's voice or style of speaking may be different from the writer's unique voice, and that's why the second-last-thing we work on is the voice or style of the fictional narrator. This is a function of language. The last technique, of course, is how to create a voice that is "unreliable." We work on details and fictional backstory, then we work on the voice or style of the fictional narrator, and finally, we work on the "unreliable narrator."*
>
> — Jack Grapes

When I started in Jack's classes, I was good at the deep voice, but I couldn't translate this over to characters. I wandered around making up characters in my head, but something got lost when I tried to write them down. Then one day Jack, said, *"Put your deep voice on the page, you know how to do that."* It was the next bit that shocked me. *"And then lie,"* he said.

> *Plato was right when he said that all poets* (meaning imaginative writers) *lie. What he failed to understand was that the sentences themselves were never false; they were the one lasting truth of art, the adventure of language.*
>
> — Jack Grapes

What Jack teaches, for writers who take the Character Class, is to write in the first person, and with each exercise, tell more and more lies. As the writer does this, the lies build on each other, and the writers experience themselves writing stories they would never have written before.

First person writing might seem counterintuitive considering we're creating character, but the more the writer focuses on the lies, the more they seem to disappear and natural characters, based part on them and part formed from the lies, begin to emerge. The week three exercise is the only week where the writer works in third person.

> *The characters in my novels are my own unrealized possibilities. That is why I am equally fond of them and equally horrified by them. Each one has crossed a border that I myself have circumnavigated.*
>
> — Milan Kundera

I don't believe that one person is more creative than another. As humans, creativity is our birthright, and our true voice is our superpower. As the great Maya Angelou said, *You cannot use up creativity. The more you use, the more you have.* If creativity builds on itself, what could you do today to kick-start your birthright of creativity?

My greatest hope is that you have some fun with this book. That you play and experiment with the exercises. That you start to see the power and brilliance of your unique creativity.

# A LITTLE ABOUT JACK GRAPES

I met Jack in 2002 when I was doing a master's program. As part of my thesis, I decided to write a book. I needed a writing teacher and a good one. I received recommendations for Jack's classes and hence my journey with Jack Grapes' Method Writing began. Little did I know back then what a pivotal part of my life Jack would become.

I was blessed to study with him for over two decades. I moved through the different levels, all the time learning more about myself as a writer and a human. I am now fortunate to teach his exercises and programs myself.

Jack is an award-winning poet, a playwright, a teacher, an actor and an editor. Over the last forty years, he has taught over three thousand poets and writers through the UCLA Extension Program and privately.

My writing and my life were never the same once I studied and practiced Jack's programs. For many years I've been thrilled to witness the same transformation happening for my students.

You will read more by Jack in the Addendum section at the end of the book.

There are those special people in our lives, and for me, Jack is one.

*Jules Swales*

# PART I

# 20% LIES—AND WHY WE DO IT

As mentioned in the Foreword, the writers in this compilation book are all Jack Grapes' Method Writing trained. They have taken at least the first two levels in my classes working with Jack's books: *Method Writing—The First Four Concepts*, and *Advanced Method Writing—The Art of Tonal Dynamics*.

For our first class, the writer is asked to write a normal journal entry (not to be confused with "journal" writing). Journal writing is more stream of consciousness, with the writer recording their thoughts and feelings from one moment to the next. The normal journal entry, by having an exercise to focus on, creates opportunities for surprises.

We cannot experience surprises, as humans or writers, if we are always doing ourselves the same way on the page, or maybe in life. "Oh my gosh! I can't believe I wrote that," is something I love to hear from students. The aim with any of the exercises is to be open to something new. *No surprise for the writer, no surprise for the reader.*—Robert Frost

In this first exercise, the writer does a simple piece of first person writing about themselves, but 20% of what they write is lies.

As you read, see if you can a) feel the voice of the writer, b) spot the lies. We never discuss what the lies are in class, which makes it more fun and enables the writer to "explore" themselves a bit more. But maybe you can spot some of the lies yourself, or at least what you think are lies.

This first week's exercise serves as a baseline. It gives the writer an opportunity to share a scene or event of their life but to lie and embellish. All good writing, even memoirs, will have a good dose of embellishment. Talking about embellishing, here's an excerpt from an interview with Vivian Gornick in *The Believer* magazine.

> *I embellish stories all the time. I do it even when I'm supposedly telling the unvarnished truth. Things happen, and I realize that what actually happens is only partly a story, and I have to make the story. So, I lie. I mean, essentially—others would think I'm lying. But you understand. It's irresistible to tell the story, and I don't owe anybody the actuality. What is actuality? I mean, whose business, is it?*

In *The Art of Memoir,* Mary Karr wrote about what she calls: The Truth Contract. In one breath she writes: *My own humble practices wholly oppose making stuff up.* But then goes on to list twelve liberties she takes, three of which are below:

1. *Shaping a narrative (which is lying). Of course, the minute you write about one thing instead of another, you've begun to leave stuff out, which you could argue is falsifying ...*

2. *Stopping to describe something in the midst of a heated scene, when I probably didn't observe it consciously at that instant. This is perhaps the biggest lie I ever tell. I do so because I am constantly trying to re-create the carnal world as I lived it, so I keep concocting an experience for the reader ...*

3. *Putting in scenes I didn't witness but only heard about … as if I were there, for a good story told often enough puts you in rooms never occupied.*

This gives you an introduction to the "why" of lying. As you read through the pieces and the introduction to each chapter you will understand and see more and more the power and creative fun in using lies and embellishment to birth character.

# A TIME TO LIVE, A TIME TO DIE
## BY FIONA JACOB

It is 06.25 on a cold November morning. I sit on the burgundy leather sofa and stare out at the grey bulbous clouds that obscure the moon and cast a yellow hue in the pre-dawn sky.

It's all quiet except for the gentle hum of the oil burner. At least I don't have to listen to the gurgle and rattle of Dad's lungs as he drowns with every breath, the CCU nurses will take care of him now.

I am angry. I am angry dad is sick. I am angry he will not live much longer. I am angry I've had to disrupt everything in my life to be here. I am angry I have to drain my finances to the bare bones to watch my parents fade into ghost-shadow versions of themselves. I am an angry, selfish cow.

This takes me back to the conversation I had yesterday at the GP practice.

"Have you thought about palliative care?" Dr Aylward said, his right eyebrow raised.

He stood tall and thin behind the wooden reception desk. The walls behind him were stark white, the LED ceiling downlights made his face look sallow. He wore beige chinos with a brown leather belt, a camel colour cashmere jumper, beige runners with brown laces. His blonde-grey hair was gelled back. He held a patient file in his left hand with 'Confidential' written in bold red letters.

I wore the same red sweater I had on for three days that smelt of stale sweat and had a coffee stain down the front. My navy trousers were covered in beige dog hairs. My unwashed hair was pulled into a ponytail with a scrunchie. A baby tooth lay on the grey lino floor beside my left foot.

I had adored Patrick Aylward when he'd been my geek teenage lover. We had reconnected five years ago at a tedious drugs anonymous meeting. Like me, he'd become an oxycodone addict after back surgery. Tears splashed down my cheeks as a blur of women with baby strollers, a wheelchair-bound woman and a young boy on crutches made quiet processions to their doctor's appointments.

"Fiona, speak to your brothers," he said in a soft voice. "It's time to pull the plug."

# THE BEST PIE EVER
## BY TRISH POMEROY

My husband was a good soul; funny, kind and smart. With blonde hair and blue eyes, he was quite the catch until he developed grumpy old man syndrome, and middle-aged years soured his personality and reduced his hairline. He wanders around the house now in his grey plaid slippers, brown corduroy jeans and ribbed knit sweater looking for his belt. I find it right where he took it off the night before. Our bedroom, once a place of fun, is now a place to sleep. Our dream home looks as tired as our love feels. The kitchen is like that of my parents, small and narrow and full of gadgets.

Mum wasn't much of a cook, you could tell what day of the week it was by the meal we had, left over cold roast meat with mash and beans on Monday; steak and kidney pie from a tin on Tuesday; mince beef and onions on Wednesday; casserole on Thursday and, of course, it was always fish on Friday, being the good Catholics we were.

My love of cooking grew as I got older. I learnt how to make choux pastry, beating in the eggs one at a time into the thick panade until the consistency was just right, or I'd rub flour and butter between my cold fingertips to make fine breadcrumbs and turn them into the flakiest puff pastry.

My husband would boast about my cooking skills. He said I was the reason he was fat and content. He worked on a building site six days a week and was always ready for a decent meal. He was sure to let it be known if it was the worst or the best meal he'd ever eaten, before he stretched out on the sofa, flicked the TV on and left me to wash up.

He said my meat pie was the best and would brag about how I would only ever make it for him.

The delicious blend of the Stilton crust and beef in gravy was divine, he'd say, as he licked the plate clean.

It was the dog's favourite meal too, minus the crust.

A large tin of dog food goes a long way.

# ODD DUCK
## BY MARY WHITE

As a seven-year-old girl, I was faced with a tough decision. Did I want to be a Brownie or a Bluebird? Brownies were the predecessor to Girl Scouts; Bluebirds, to Camp Fire Girls. My mom chose Bluebirds as they were less stringent and cheaper. I liked the Bluebird uniform, red vests, navy skirts and red neck ties, better than the drab "brown" Brownie attire. I attended the Bluebird troop meetings held in the basement of my elementary school. Being outgoing and a bit of an entertainer, I relished the camaraderie and soaked up the attention.

Several months passed and I still didn't have my uniform. All the other Bluebirds wore theirs to the meetings. I looked like I didn't belong.

One meeting, the leader shared that our troop was going to be on TV. I panicked. After school, I ran to my mom and told her the news, begging for my uniform. She gave me a blank stare and said, "yes, yes, we'll get to that." I waited for weeks then demanded to know about the uniform. "We are not going to buy you a uniform. You will have to wear this sundress. It is adorable on you," she said, as she held up my bright pink sundress covered with white and yellow daisies. No words could escape my clenched throat. My face prickled hot. I started to cry but she didn't notice. We sat in my parents' bedroom on one of two double beds covered with white spreads. Between the beds stood a taupe nightstand with a brass lamp, alarm clock, and ashtray, half full. The room smelled of stale cigarette smoke, cologne and hair spray. My mom had fine, permed, ash-blond hair, and pale blue eyes. Red lipstick tinted her lips and distracted from her saggy chin. Dressed for spring, she wore a striped navy and white shirt and navy slacks. I felt the unnatural texture of the gold shag carpet under my bare feet. A blue pill lay on the floor near the dresser. "But everyone else will be in red and navy uniforms on TV!" I said. "I will be the odd duck in pink!" "You will be adorable," she said.

# THE HOMECOMING
## BY KRYSTEEN DVORACEK

My daughter Miranda says I have the right to wear things that make me feel good. She's promised to take me clothes shopping for my sixtieth birthday so I can explore a new look. Not for work. Not for yoga or the gym. Not for anyone else, just for me. I haven't expressed myself through my clothes for a long time. Not since I was a teenager.

"What happened to all my Greville Street vintage clothes?" I said. I'd just finished pulling out the contents of my tiny wardrobe. It held just a few pairs of jeans and tops, nothing special, nothing I liked. My skin was pale and my eyes red rimmed from jet lag. I was fifteen and I'd flown in from Bangkok the day before, back from a Rotary student exchange program. My bedroom smelt stale. Dried cat shit poked out from under the bed.

Mum stood in the doorway, her large, red, swollen hands resting at her hips. Brown eyes framed by thick bushy eyebrows stared blankly at me. Folds of flesh bulged against the cotton of her uniform, stained from a day serving customers in the family butcher shop. I couldn't find my beautiful fawn crêpe de Chine dress, the one with the delicate brown beading on the pocket. I couldn't find my pleated floral violet dress with the nipped-in waist. I couldn't find the diagonal skirt I'd hand-sewn from silk scarves, the one I'd twirl in like a princess.

Mum had watched me search without saying a word. She shrugged and said: "I didn't think you'd want them when you came back, so I threw them out." No point arguing. I'd learnt that as a child. Mum had a venomous tongue that sought out drama. Me getting upset just lit a match to her kindling and she loved a good blaze. She'd blaze for hours, before turning into ash. I'd started buying my own clothes at thirteen, vintage bargains. My best friend's mum used to take her clothes shopping. That was never going to happen with us. I'd earned the money to buy every piece of vintage clothing I had. Now it was gone. I'd been gone for a year, but nothing at home had changed. Mum was still mum, and that was that.

# I LONGED FOR A PAST THAT DIDN'T EXIST
## BY TSILAH BURMAN

I am a mess. I need to keep moving, to dissociate, to escape the present moment and the denseness in my head. I live in terror. I long for the joy I felt as a child—carefree and embraced. I reach for peace and pull out a withered hand filled with crab-apples.

"I want ice cream," I said. We were in Israel at a museum amongst the caramel-colored cliffs of the Golan. A painting, behind an overturned jeep—the remnants of the 1967, Six-Day War—showed an outstretched arm pushing the Israelis into the sea to drown them. My mom wore a muumuu-type dress in multi-shades of blue. My dad wore a green, white and black Hawaiian print short-sleeve shirt over navy blue shorts. The scent of falafel from the cafeteria filled the building. My parents stood next to me in the heat of an argument. A Hebrew Bazooka gum comic was crumpled near my mother's foot. A camera hung around my dad's neck. The air in the museum was oppressive. "Did you hear me?" I said.

I was invisible amidst the warring factions. I needed to take a side. On one side, my dad with his quirky Jerry Lewis personality. On the other side, my mother who was there for everyone but herself and my dad. There was a constant storm at sea, so it was smarter to be quiet and not make any more waves. In the middle of turmoil, I only had food to quell my emotions. And the sweeter and carbier, the better. Ice cream, brownies, and carrot kugel were some of my favorites.

I could always puke the excess up after.

I longed for a past that didn't exist. Now I've let go of the past that wasn't and the past that was. I live in the here and now. I no longer stew over what I missed or dream about a fairy-tale future which I didn't believe I deserved.

A quiet calm embraces me and fills me with awe. I've made peace with the present. I'm comfortable not knowing. I let the universe bring what it will.

# LUCKY TO BE ALIVE
## BY BIANCA BAZIN

There is no feeling so terrifying and electrifying as not being able to breathe. The gasp, the gulp, the desperate choke for the air that has been cleaved from your lungs as it renders you frantic, thrashing, shaking, desperate.

Breathing never came easily to me, despite its essentiality. My very introduction to this world was by strangulation; my umbilical cord wrapped and tangled itself around my tiny neck. The doctors said I was lucky to be alive. I often wonder which was the lucky part.

The second time, I was ten years old, and my sister found an undisclosed humour in holding me beneath the water in the pool on a family holiday in France. I still remember my cheap yellow bikini strings floating by my hips, my flailing arms grabbing at the sky, and the warped sound of her laughter from above the water's edge.

A little older, once I had grown out of my childhood asthma, I was walking back to my asbestos-ridden student accommodation at university, back to my flatmates who bullied me, a boyfriend who disgusted me and a message from the man who raped me two years prior, when I keeled over as my lungs refused to expand. The weight of an ocean submerged my body in an instant, bringing me to my knees. Alone on an empty pavement with no one there to release me. For months, this pattern played on repeat, the same empty street corner, the same collapsed and asphyxiated me.

At twenty-six years of age, I got into a relationship with a man who liked to play rough in bed. He asked me to experiment, which I discovered came with scrapes and the occasional tear. I often awoke strapped to a bedpost, naked, and gagged. His hand clenched around my throat while it pumped, controlling my airflow, until he decided I'd had enough. I'd thrash and tug at the ties as the blood swelled around my bloodshot eyes. His gaze never left mine until he climaxed and expelled me from his grip. I stayed in that relationship for five years. Why? It's when I stop breathing, I remember, I am lucky to be alive.

# A CHILD'S DESPAIR
## BY HILDA RHODES

Air bubbles floated towards the surface in a crazy dance. My nine-year-old arms thrashed like limp spaghetti in the chlorinated water. My panicked brain knew my feet should not be above my head. A desperate prayer formed amidst the nauseous fear. I prayed someone in the crowded swimming pool would notice my feet sticking up through a blue plastic ring that floated on the surface of the pool.

No one had been paying attention to me. Pushing the plastic ring under the surface to take it off feet first, had been something fun to try. I was shocked when I flipped upside down. I'd gulped water. My nostrils had burned from the chlorine infused water. A dark red mist began to cloud my consciousness. I felt my bottom bump the bottom of the pool. I sank into a deep nothingness, a still quietness; but it wasn't my time. The laws of nature pushed me to the surface. Snot and water spluttered from my nose and mouth. I shook my head. The noise of the crowded swimming pool exploded in my ears.

"Dad!" I shrieked. My dad didn't hear. The dark hair on the back of his head was slick and shiny with water. Fine black hairs clung to the wet white skin of his shoulders. A red plastic pencil sharpener floated on the surface of the water next to his outstretched left arm. My big sister had her hands on his shoulders. The dark blue rubber swim cap stretched over her hair, outlining her delicate pink face. Droplets of water clung to her long eyelashes. Her blue eyes sparkled as she bobbed up and down in the shimmering water smiling, laughing. She didn't have a ring, she could swim. Tears of jealousy burned my eyes. Dad turned around. "Time to go home," he said. I nodded. Nobody had noticed my struggle under the surface, nobody had missed me, nobody had noticed my tears, nobody loved me.

My dad and my sister chatted and laughed on the bus going home. Nobody noticed I was quiet, nobody noticed the blood that dribbled from my clenched fist. The sharp edge of the red plastic pencil sharpener had cut into my palm.

# IN MY HEAD
## BY MARGO GEORGE

Inside my head lives an insane woman. I call her my whacko. She shows up when she feels like it. On the outside, I turn into a reactive and stressed mess. I don't know her, but she knows me well. She takes me over, runs me ragged, speaks for me, acts for me, throws a tantrum for me.

This dark shadow rises. I lose control. I get obliterated. Invisible tears stream down my face and inside I scream a banshee's mournful wail. My eardrums are battered. My nerves are in tatters. I cannot hear my husband speak. He talks, but I am not there. All he sees of me is an empty shell that sucks on sherbet lemon sweets and nods in agreement. He doesn't notice and continues to spurt unrecognisable babble.

My husband, Robert, is oblivious to my whacko, as he creates a lentil roast for Sunday dinner, with mashed potatoes and steamed asparagus. A feast prepared and served to me. We each have our jobs now that the kids have grown up and left home. I clean, he cooks, he shops, he gardens. I let him. I feel moments of guilt, they pass quick.

Since he was ill with cancer five years ago, he has been at home every day. He takes care of me, to make up for years of workaholism and his own absence in life.

I go from one obsession to the next and squander each away. My whacko consumes me, and I am lost. I can't show up in my life. I act my way through each day and miss the moments which I long to replay.

I listen to podcasts, books and watch video clips in a desperate pursuit to purge my whacko. I know it won't work. Despite my endeavours, I don't want to give her up. I feed my whacko a gourmet meal, and a tornado evolves. The evening arrives, this whirlwind settles. Puff and she is gone, the calm after the storm. She returns soon. She will not let me forget her.

# NOT BORING
## BY CHRISTINE MANDER

It's raining and windy. I've just turned the music off, so the room sounds very quiet, apart from the dripping and whooshing outside. I went to the library earlier on. I love watching people more than I like talking to them. The library has long tables, so I was able to sit with people, listening to their conversations. I sat next to a group of four elderly women. I learnt about their trips to Blackpool. I learnt how one of them hates shopping for clothes, because she never likes how they look on her. The same lady had lost her keys. I could sense she was the one they had to look after, to encourage and to calm. Their talk turned to cruises.

I hated the cruise I went on. I spent most of it avoiding the person I'd sat next to on the first night. There were too many people squashed into a small space and no escape. Even on the trips ashore, I kept bumping into the same people, listening to them complain about the food and the customs of the locals.

I wonder if people look at me and think, there's an elderly person, a lonely elderly person, writing in her book. It's not how I think of myself but who knows. I remember a time, many years ago, when I joined a Quaker meeting. I was going to a house group for the first time. I walked in and sat down.

The room was cosy, with floral curtains and patterned sofas. A long low table was in front of the sofa, with biscuits and cakes and cups and saucers. I was the youngest person in the room by a long way and everyone seemed to know everyone else apart from me. It was a winter night, so the curtains were closed. A forgotten paper clip lay under one of the chairs. What am I doing here? I thought, surrounded by all these dull old people. Then the sharing and conversation started. "You were at Greenham Common, weren't you?" one of the women asked her neighbour. "Yes and I went to prison for a while. I met some fascinating people in Holloway."

# PART II

# 50% LIES

This week, the writer extends the quantity of lies to 50%, which equates to half of the writing. As they do this, they start to see how the lies impact and shift not only what they write, but also how they are writing.

Within the 50% lies they write two expositional lies, as in facts about their life. Where they were born, or raised, where they went to school, did someone die, their marital situation, did they move a lot as a child or adult, and maybe they lie about what their parents did for work, etc. They also include two event or significant object lies. A car explosion, their first kiss, or how they kept a 4.25 mm Liliput pistol in their nightstand drawer, next to a bible, and that first time they used it.

It has always been amazing to me that once a writer is given permission to lie, and they do it, there is an immediate shift in what is available to them creatively. The "wanting to be good," loosens its grip on page performance. They settle in a bit, and have fun even. That's the beauty of creativity, it grows and shapes us, the more we grow and shape ourselves.

During class there is always one student who says, *I'm not a liar, I pride myself in being honest and telling the truth.* Sigh. *No, you are a liar.* We all are. When was the last time you said *I'm fine*, when you weren't fine? Or *I love you,* when you didn't, when you faked an orgasm, stayed friends with someone you no longer like, or don't set boundaries for yourself? Lying is subtle and, in some form or other, we do it all the time. Get over yourself, I say, and get creating.

> *Sanity is a cozy lie.*
> — Susan Sontag

> *One can be absolutely truthful and sincere even though admittedly the most outrageous liar. Fiction and invention are the very fabric of life.*
> — Henry Miller

Coming back, for a second, to the last chapter's introduction. Whatever the form, or genre, one's own voice is the motor that drives the truth of the character. Nobody else has your truth. And your truth, your voice, is the center point of everything you write.

When we write, tell lies even, we are attempting to show a feeling. It is the depth of our ability to show feeling that connects with the reader. They want to forget about you as the writer and find themselves in your world and in your words.

This is ever-present in James Joyce's books, *Ulysses, Dubliners,* and *Portrait of The Artist as a Young Man,* where he has similar characters in different fictional stories. The same with all of Jane Austen's novels. Were they characters, or were they in fact part of Joyce or Austen themselves? The answer is both Yes and Yes.

# IT'S NO SURPRISE I'M SINGLE
## BY TSILAH BURMAN

Men have disappointed me my whole life. My dad, loud and obnoxious, was the first. I looked like him. Red hair, a round face, and a glint in the eyes. He would yell our friends' names in strange ways, elongating syllables that didn't exist. I cringed when embarrassment followed for them and my older brother. My dad would go into people's homes and look in their drawers and cabinets. He collected pinball machines which were lined up in our enclosed patio. After my brother and I moved out, my dad would invite young religious kids from the neighborhood to come over and play pinball. At my sixth-grade graduation party, at our house, I was mortified when my father organized a game of Spin the Bottle. My mother was in the kitchen entertaining the parents of one of the girls in my class and had no idea what my father had done. Shame ran through my veins and colored my world.

My brother was the second guy to disappoint me. I looked up to him. He was tall, smart and good-looking. I was short, stupid and fat. I was jealous of his popularity and how everything came easy to him. He was a wiz at math and science, while I got caught cheating on a test because I didn't know my multiplication tables. He teased me that he had a higher IQ than me.

I started young, trying to prove myself and show the world I was better than how I felt.

Later, my brother dropped out of med school, traveled to India and joined an ashram. I was the opposite, a straight arrow, gripping for control and shattered by my brother's fall from grace in my eyes.

Both my dad and brother were stinging Scorpios. I decided to avoid Scorpio men and even went to the extreme of not having sex in February and March when I was trying to get pregnant.

I didn't look at myself. It's no surprise I'm single.

# STRANGE CHARACTERS
## BY CHRISTINE MANDER

I'm sitting in the kitchen of my friend's Norfolk cottage. I'm calm and feel very much at peace. I'm thinking a lot about my family, remembering the times we spent together, remembering how I used to be as a child before life toughened me up.

My parents took me and my sister to Disneyland when I was six and my sister eight. I was a very nervous child and thought too much. I found the outsize characters terrifying. Who was the person behind the Mickey Mouse costume? What did they really look like? Even Snow White, the closest to a normal human, frightened me. She was too good to be true.

We were sitting down to lunch and an enormous Pluto sat down beside me. His costume stank of stale cigarettes and body odour. Close up it was stained and torn. He was trying to be playful with me and my sister, but he was a little off key. Perhaps he didn't work there and had just brought his own costume. Even at six, or maybe especially at six, I feared the worst.

My sister took everything at face value, so for her it was all fun. No monsters under her bed or ghouls hiding in the wardrobe. I envied her that freedom. The freedom not to make pictures of the worst thing that might happen. In my head I'd already been abducted by the rogue Pluto and locked in the trunk of his ancient car, but she was happily chatting away to him.

My mum sort of understood my fears, but her way of comforting me was to tell me how she had been the same when she was a child. Sadly, this had the opposite effect, making me feel doomed to repeat her experiences. At least she didn't panic and attempt to send me to a psychiatrist, as a mother might today. Years later she told me that she had mentioned one of my strange behaviours to the local doctor. I had an obsession where if I scratched something I might have damaged it and had to tell my Mum every time. Fortunately, the doctor was sensible enough to say, "don't worry she'll grow out of it."

# BROKEN WIDOW

## BY MARGO GEORGE

My husband's cancer hit me hard. I didn't think it would happen to me. In one pivotal moment, life tested me. I failed. My husband might die. I could be a widow. My four kids would have no father. I didn't know if I could do the eulogy or plan the funeral. I am not creative like that. I wouldn't do him justice. He is the tough one. I am the hanger on.

I wore the armour of a strong independent woman; inside I was putty. When touched with a feather I collapsed in a heap. A pendulum between tenacious and chaotic, life often felt like a car wreck.

Four weeks after a lesion was discovered in my husband's rectum, we sat before the Consultant. He dealt us a partial card on each visit, one titbit at a time, over what was to be eighteen months of treatment. It was a slow march through hell. The consultant took pleasure from being positive about disaster. My husband mirrored his response with pleasant banter about a small matter of an out-of-control cancerous growth. As they laughed and got to know each other, I was a broken widow with four young children, at forty, on Plenty of Fish in search for a new husband. I'd have to learn how to put water in my car, hang a picture frame, keep a plant alive, deal with the accountant that would be right in there to nab a rich widow. I needed another accountant before my husband died.

Robert's demeanour was admirable, even when he had six weeks of radiotherapy, life changing surgery to remove his rectum and six months of the highest chemotherapy he could handle without going into toxic overload.

He lost it once. When he discovered he would be left with a permanent stoma, he got fixated on the fact the stoma nurse said he would never be able to wear a belt on his trousers. I was in meltdown. I envisaged his stoma explode, poo everywhere, in the lounge of The Ritz, and he was worried about his leather belt. My husband was at a fashion show, the stoma nurse was clueless and yet again I was living in a nightmare.

## PIGS MIGHT FLY
### BY HILDA RHODES

The rain pelted at the kitchen window. I stared at the bowl of dull grey porridge. The milk puddled in little white circles across its surface. I closed my eyes. The whirl of sun, sandy beaches, loud music, and drunken parties flitted through my head, the holiday in Mallorca. My friends had invited me because my original plans had been wrecked by my boyfriend dumping me. On holiday I'd drowned my sorrows in alcohol. I'd been drunk and careless. I got pregnant. At eighteen I was about to start my second year at Glasgow University. Too terrified to tell anyone, especially my parents, I'd had a backstreet abortion. I felt giddy. I clenched my teeth as excruciating pain shot through my belly.

"Dad, I need to tell you something," I said. My dad and I sat at the yellow Formica-topped table in the cramped kitchen. It was pushed against the wall. A half empty milk bottle, a bowl of white sugar, an open pot of my Mum's raspberry jam and a dead wasp were clustered in the centre of the table. Pink and white spotted baby-doll pyjamas stuck to my clammy skin under a pink flannelette dressing gown. Lank, greasy strands of fair hair hung over my hunched shoulders. Dark shadows had formed under my dull eyes. Yellow headed pimples dotted my forehead. "I've had an abortion," I said.

Dad was reading last night's *Evening Times*. A small tube of travel toothpaste which was a free gift with the newspaper, lay next to his mug of instant coffee. My heart was pounding in my chest. He turned towards me without putting down his newspaper. I looked into his eyes expecting to see some sort of emotion, but his pale grey eyes gave me nothing. His expression was as bland as the yellow painted wall opposite him. "If you tell your mother I will never speak to you again," he said.

I had decided to tell my dad in hopes he would be concerned. Maybe he would understand. Maybe he'd have compassion. Maybe we'd tell Mum together. Maybe pigs might fly!

# STACCATO DANCER
## BY KRYSTEEN DVORACEK

Today I drove to Castlemaine to dance. It had taken me six months to show up to dance with the local Five Rhythms community. I wore my light grey wool leggings and my sparkly green ring for luck. Jewellery wasn't welcome on the dance floor, but I wore it anyway, my birthstone, to give me courage.

I saw an open door and walked up the stairs at the side of St Mary's Church hall. The door at the top was open. I headed in. People were seated in a semicircle on green, fake leather upholstered seats, grouped around the lectern at the front. My eyes fixed on one man. Sitting alone, hunched over with his head in his hands, bowed shoulders, tension in every muscle. Tapping his leg, over and over, in a dark staccato rhythm on the floor.

"AA meeting, love," said the man at the door. "Them dancers are downstairs. I'm guessing that's who you want?"

He was right. I wanted the dancers. But I knew the drinkers. I'd sat in halls like this, sobbing into my hands. Wanting to be dead but knowing I couldn't do that to my son. It would have been like tying a rock to his chest before I chucked him in the river. I wanted to chuck myself in so bad back then, back when

I was a drinker. Back when I was thirty-five and he was five. Today I'm sixty-five, and I'm a dancer.

When I got downstairs there was a young mum and her five-year-old son dancing together. My eyes were riveted. He climbed on her legs, swung from her arms, crazy acrobats together. The community danced around them, sharing the joy in their play. I wanted to share the joy, but I couldn't. Sobs rose inside me at what I'd gone and wasted. Precious years I could have danced with my son. I was drunk instead.

I danced my sobs in staccato. Shook and shook them out of my body. Forced them from my fingers in violent thrusts. Shook my legs and stamped my feet. Pounded out the sorrow until it was empty, and I was empty. Spent like an empty whisky bottle. No going back.

# THE ACCUSED
## BY FIONA JACOB

"Has the jury reached a verdict?" the judge said to the jury foreman in a measured gravel voice.

We stood in Crown courtroom three, a towering ancient mausoleum with vaulted cathedral ceilings, domed windows, white plastered walls, and dark lacquered wooden benches. Narrow slivers of feeble spring sunlight shone through the windows and illuminated dust particles that floated in the hushed courtroom air.

The judge, a thick-jowled man in his sixties with puffy eyes and deep grooves in his cheek-folds, leaned forward on his maroon leather chair. He wore a short bench wig, black and lilac silks, a red sash across his corpulent belly and a stiff white jabot at his throat. A gold-plated royal coat of arms hung on the wall behind him. His face was impassive.

Paul, the accused, flanked by two bored prison guards, stood ramrod tall in the glass dock. He wore a dark navy suit that hung on him like a wire coat hanger. His crisp white shirt and muted navy and grey tie made his gaunt face look ashen. His short salt and pepper spiked hair was reminiscent of an aging punk rocker. A distinguished flying cross was pinned to his suit with a white and purple striped ribbon. The gold wedding band on his left ring finger was loose.

On the prosecuting barrister's table, an eight-inch kitchen knife covered with dried blood was sheathed in a clear evidence bag with a bright red seal and marked exhibit number one.

Kate, my friend, and I stood side by side and faced the judge. My heart pounded and my armpits were damp underneath my red Armani trouser suit and cream silk blouse. My feet ached in Jimmy Choo stilettos. Beside my right foot, a broken wooden toothpick lay on the ground. I traced my fingers along the tender white scar ridge on my right-hand palm. Kate chewed the inside of her mouth and stared straight ahead.

"My lord," the tattooed foreman said in a Jamaican accent. "We, the jury, find the defendant, Paul Ridley, guilty on two counts of attempted murder."

Paul bowed his head. I dissolved in tears. Kate screeched like a feral animal.

Her husband, the hero psychopath, could never hurt us again.

# HALF-READ BOOKS
## BY TRISH POMEROY

I don't care that my wardrobe is no longer organised by colour, season, or purpose or that there always seems to be a pile of half-read books by my bed. One day, I will publish a book of my own that will end up in a pile of other half-read books by someone else's bed.

As a child, I switched the lights back on to read, long after everyone had gone to bed, or I hid in the wardrobe so no one could find me. I sat with a torch in one hand and a book in the other, amongst the piles of shoes and clothes hanging overhead. I lost myself between the pages of romance or horror, fantasy, and fiction.

I imagined myself as a heroine saving the world from death and destruction, or as a noble queen ruling my kingdom with pride, always on the search for my prince and true love.

I made up story books, drawing pictures and binding the paper by sewing the edges together with wool.

I sold them to friends and family and used the money to buy more colouring pens and paper, much to my aunt's delight.

"You're such a good storyteller," my Aunt Mabel said.

She was a teacher and always looked smart in her cream blouse with cornflower blue buttons and a lace trimmed collar, matched with a skirt pleated to perfection. Her grey hair was tied up and pinned to her head in a neat bun, tortoiseshell reading glasses perched on the edge of her nose as she held my book in her wrinkled old hands. We sat in her lounge on her yellow and brown floral sofa next to the overfilled and dust-layered bookcase. The grandfather clock ticked in the background and the dining room table held the remains of dead flowers in a vase. A baked bean remained from yesterday's dinner.

"Thank you," I said.

Inside, my heart beamed with pride. I adored my aunt, so full of knowledge and wise.

I threw away her wisdom when I threw away my books with the rest of my childhood. I threw away the wrong types of clutter.

# DEATH OF A DREAM
## BY MARY WHITE

Piano was my first love. I picked out nursery rhymes around age three. By seven or eight, I'd learned many tunes from my babysitter. I overheard my parents say I had an ear for music. My dad and I played duets together, me sitting to his right, noodling out the melody or accompaniment to songs like "Honeysuckle Rose" or "Sweet Georgia Brown". He was patient, kind and never critical. When I missed a note, he would let out a chuckle and say, "don't worry, you can't get it wrong with jazz!" When I played well, he would exclaim, "fantasmagloria," a word his father invented. At age nine, I began classical lessons with a stellar pianist and Juilliard graduate. I learned to play Chopin, Bach and Mozart. When I was sixteen, I played Chopin's Prelude in D-flat Major with my music book closed. I knew the music down to my cells. My teacher gave me a standing ovation. A friend's mother told me I was brave to play without the music, to which I replied that the written notes would have been a distraction. I played with my blood, from the depth of my being.

After I graduated high school, I was accepted into the Juilliard School in New York for piano performance and composition. I floated through school, stunned that my dream of being a composer and performer was being realized.

But fate had other plans. A fellow student and I went to dinner for my birthday. On the way back we were separated, and I got mugged on the subway platform. Never one to be passive, I fought off my mugger who sliced my right hand with a knife and knocked me out. I woke up in the hospital with a bandaged hand and a grim prognosis. My ulnar nerve was severed and required surgery. After weeks of recovery, I could only use my left hand for piano. My right pinky lost its power, and the scar tissue made it painful to play octaves. I was shattered. I drifted and found solace in drugs with other lost souls. I never reclaimed the discipline to continue my studies and only dabbled with piano from then on. It was the death of a dream.

# I WISH HE'D CALLED ME A CUNT
## BY BIANCA BAZIN

My fingers are as wrinkled as a cat's puckered arsehole. I've been lying in the bath for three hours now, flicking the hot tap on and off with my big toe to stop me from freezing. No matter how much I soak and scrub, I can't peel the grime from my skin. I'm drenched in my own filth.

You see, my husband, John, and I have been bad for a while. Well, more like as stale as a Victorian prisoner's supper, and in a moment of weakness, I choked, and I cheated. I'd blame the red wine, but really, I'm just a pathetic piece of dog shit smeared on your new suede shoes. Now, John's no saint either; I've seen the lies, the wandering eyes and hushed phone calls behind closed doors. He loved me once, I'm sure. He'd leave me handwritten notes while I slept and buy me flowers just because it was Friday. But somewhere along the love line where our palms met, we shattered.

I thought a baby would solve everything. A pure, innocent soul we could pour our love into, and by consequence, remember how to love each other. No child would want to be born to my shallow, cobwebbed womb. I strangled the seed with my desperation long before it had the chance to bloom. It abandoned me as a sticky congealed blob that oozed out the sides of my black-laced thong and dribbled down my thighs crying, "Mayday! This wretch doesn't deserve the name mum!" I never told John about the baby. I flushed my secret down the drain, hoping with time the stench of my barren heart would decay.

When I told John of my infidelity, I thought he would forgive, that he would recognise my vain attempt to regain his affection, and finally we could lick our wounds and heal. I was fooling myself. Instead, I gave him the reason he'd been looking for to cut and run. He didn't get mad or even look surprised, instead his greyish-blue eyes fixed on the door. Without even a flinch he said, "We're done." It would have hurt less if he'd called me a cunt.

# PART III

# JACK GRAPES' CHARACTER TEMPLATE©—CHARACTER DATE

Now for something different. There are two assignments for the third week of class.

For the first assignment the writer prints out their Jack Grapes' Character Template. You will see the checklists as you read the chapter. And they take themselves out on a Character Date.

The writer takes some printed checklists, a notepad, plus some favorite pens and puts themself in a place where they can watch people, even if they stay in their car. They watch how people walk, what they are wearing, their mannerisms, etc.

Then they pick two people and fill out a Character Template for each of them. They make up all sorts of things about the people they have chosen. This is another awesome way to build character. As humans, we move so fast, and we miss so much. This exercise teaches us to be more curious about the world around us.

I take little 3 x 5 note cards when I go on Character Dates. Once I went to the park. There was a woman on a bench. She wore a navy suit, had blonde hair in a tight bun, and sat on her own, eating a pre-packaged salad. I wrote all sorts of expositional facts about her, how she hated her job as a doctor. I made notes about the car she drove, a Bronco truck, I thought. And that she and her husband, who was a mechanic, had motorbikes, and they tinkered with them every Sunday, while she, earbuds in her ears, listened to podcasts on how to date women.

I wrote my second checklist for a security guard who was driving around the park. He was super wealthy and had always wanted to be a cop, but was too old, hence the security job. He had aphenphosmphobia (fear of being touched), something about his overcrowded childhood. I filled notecards about them both, and a Character Template.

Second Assignment: Pick one of the two people they did a template for and write a piece about them in either third person, (as in he, she, it, him, his, her), or first person (which is I, me, we, us, mine, our, and us). The writer will use the information from the template to dive into a narrative, all made up, about who this person is.

When reading this you can either read the narrative piece first and the template after, or read the template first. You will see how the writer took information from the template as a sort of framework. But also, and let's not forget this, everything that the writer sees in the other person, in that stranger in the park or grocery store, in some way or another, lives inside the writer also, either as a fear, a dream, a loathing, or a love. The eyes with which we see the world show us reflections of our own self. Everything we see, everything we love or dislike in others is always alive within ourselves.

> Psychological Projection: A type of defence mechanism in which a person, consciously or unconsciously, attributes their own thoughts, feelings, or traits onto another person or group.
> — *Forbes Health*

One of the things I hear most from the writer after their Character Date, is that they couldn't believe how much they noticed around them and in people. Followed by variations of this: *How come I don't see all this when I'm not doing a writing exercise?* Or, *I noticed that I don't look around me as I go through life.* And most common, *I think I live on automatic.*

# CHARACTER TEMPLATE

## NO BEEF

**Physical Info:**

Female mid-30s. Slim, athletic, brown hair that she has dyed blonde. Perfect figure, teeth, and eyesight.

**Expositional Facts:**

Born in Singapore but grew up in America, and now lives in Dubai. She is an only child. Her parents were middle class but taught her to like and aim for the finer things in life. Heartbroken by her sweetheart who cheated on her in college.

**Occupation:**

Works in a 5-star hotel in Dubai as part of the banqueting team. Manages the bar and has ambitions of being the hotel manager. She moved back to Singapore after graduating college and waited tables before moving to work behind the bar. She worked in an ice cream bar when in college.

**Habits:**

Intermittent fasting, 17 hours without food, 3 days a week. Is addicted to staying thin, exercises all the time, and drives fast in her very old convertible Mercedes.

**Hobbies:**

Loves watching light hopeful movies. "The Devil Wears Prada" is her favourite and she has watched it 67 times to date. She likes expensive clothes, but her budget doesn't allow, so she buys fake designer clothes and accessories.

## Phobias:
Germaphobia, mysophobia – fear of germs. She is always cleaning, has 3 packets of anti-bacterial wipes in her car. Will not use a public toilet.

## Temperament:
Happy-go-lucky person, always smiling. Guests and management love her. Can be bossy towards staff who work for her. One minute praising them the next telling them off. Smiles when talking to customers then curses them behind their back.

## Traumas/Unusual Compulsions:
Got locked in a cow shed as a child and has hated cows since. Has abandonment issues after her last boyfriend betrayed her. Hates American men.

## Food Preferences:
Love fish, hates beef. Favorite meal is shrimp and salad. Loves white wine.

## What is in their fridge/medicine cabinet:
Fridge: Soya and Oat milk, sparkling water, cans of kombucha. 1.5 bottles of Italian white wine. Out-of-date bag of spinach, feta cheese, and a pack of tofu.
Medicine cabinet: multivitamins, Sudocrem. Blue plasters stolen from work. Nail scissors, out-of-date condom.

*Trish Pomeroy*

# NO BEEF
## BY TRISH POMEROY

Lili woke up at 5 am, showered and dressed herself in sweatpants, sports bra, and a skimpy orange sports top that matched her trainers. She popped the roof down on her third-hand red Maserati. She checked herself in the mirror, as she put on her fake Dior sunglasses to shield her brown eyes from the sun. She smiled as she admired her reflection.

Despite the early hour, the sun felt warm as she sped down the highway. She arrived at the parking lot of the gym, put her sunglasses in the glove compartment, raised the roof and locked the car. Once inside, she headed to the treadmill. She needed to burn off some energy. She needed to run. She needed to escape the longing that was stirred inside her. She longed for love, but lovers were for losers.

The news was on in the background, and she ran her way through the talk of riots, floods and corrupt presidents. She admired the male news reader and wondered if his body was toned underneath his white shirt and blue suit. The door to the gym opened and in walked a blonde American guy. She knew he was American, as she often heard him talking out loud to his PT instructor. Today was no different.

"I am in the mood to pump some iron," he said.

He wore a grey sweat top with the word **Harvard** on the front, black shorts, white trainers, and white socks. His blue eyes looked bright against his tanned, muscular skin. His legs spread wide across the black mat, the weighted bar by his feet. The personal trainer stood by his side. She had a small frame, a plain face, and cropped black hair. A tiny piece of tissue paper stuck to her shoe. The wall behind them had mirrored glass with a water cooler in the corner, next to the Fire Exit door.

"You need to shut up," Lili said to him in her head.

He reminded her of the guy she served in the bar last night, an American tourist, all talk, and no substance. She watched as his big mouth wrapped around the rare beefburger and fat dripped down his double chin.

"I'm in the mood to pump some beef today," he said as he winked in her direction. "You ready for some action, honey?"

She laughed as she poured a small amount of arsenic into his bourbon.

# CHARACTER TEMPLATE
## KOOKABURRA SWOOPS

**Physical Info:**
An older woman, in her late 70s. Grey short hair, square face, large plastic-rimmed glasses. She walks slowly and with deliberateness. Like she is afraid to fall.

**Expositional Facts:**
Raised in Melbourne, Australia. Went to a posh Anglican grammar school. Dad was a surgeon. Mom stayed at home to raise her and her younger brother. Only traveled once, to England after her father died. She is single, no children.

**Occupation:**
Was a librarian because she loved books. She didn't like dealing with the people in the library but loved to catalog and restore the old books.

**Habits:**
Drives a vintage navy-blue Jaguar. Wears eccentric, quirky clothes. Lives alone in a large stately home she inherited. Collects stones and small rocks.

**Hobbies:**
Bird watching, hiking, gardening, music (loves the Rolling Stones). Listens to ABC classic radio. Likes to keep a count of how many hours/days she can go without talking to another human. Walking with her dog.

**Phobias:**
Androphobia—fear of men. Enochlophobia—fear of crowds.

**Temperament:**
Shy. Timid. Nervous around other humans.

**Traumas/Unusual Compulsions:**
Feels unloved/unlovable. Mom was emotionally distant putting father always first. Wants to always be in control. Father always wanted a boy and let her know that. She is scared of rejection, so she doesn't let anyone close.

**Food Preferences:**
Porridge every morning with cream and sugar. Loves meat and makes a mean lamb roast. Has toast and bitter marmalade for lunch with strong black tea.

**What is in their fridge/medicine cabinet:**
Fridge: Full-fat milk. Butter. Meat for her and the dog. Marmalade. A week-old lasagna, an English cucumber, two bars of dark chocolate, and a bottle of wine.
Medicine cabinet: St. John's Wort to help her sleep. Aspirin. Betadine, Band-Aids, and bandages. A knee brace.

*Krysteen Dvoracek*

## KOOKABURRA SWOOPS
### BY KRYSTEEN DVORACEK

I felt so tired it hurt my face. All that effort just to keep my eyes open. The late morning sun made my grey and pink wool skirt so hot; it scorched my bare legs. I still had on my hiking boots, red socks and hat from this morning's walk. It would have been so easy to let go. To snooze. Instead, part of me stayed alert, watching.

I sat in the white wicker chair facing the formal lawn of our Macedon home. The garden table was set with a white china teapot with proper leaf tea and four triangles of bitter marmalade toast. Ziggy, my rescue greyhound, lay sprawled on the grass, snoring. She still startles easily.

Late morning, dog walked, tea made. I sat alone in the garden and listened to layers of birdsong and soaked in the beauty of the last burgundy roses and the falling leaves of the claret ash. I regretted not becoming a landscape gardener. Dad said girls became teachers or nurses or, since I loved books, I could become a librarian. So I did. I loved to catalogue, alone.

A Kookaburra swooped down from the big old gum next to the gate and pecked hard at the grass. Fast, so the worm wouldn't have seen it coming. Big, showy birds with wide, blue-tipped wings and a raucous laugh. Kookaburras were never my favourite. I favoured the fairy wrens that darted through the scrub, almost invisible unless you looked hard.

Today is Anzac Day. I missed the dawn service for the first time in seventy years. I couldn't bear the crowds. I remember how proud I was, that first Anzac Day parade march as a seven-year-old girl. How dad marched, stiff and slow. He'd been a prisoner on the Thai Burma Railway. I don't need to go somewhere to remember him.

I wish he could have loved me more. I remember how when I was a child, he used to go off his nut. I'd do something to upset him, and he'd scream. His face would be so big and white and angry. Loud, up close, in my face. He never spoke about the Railway. Instead, he'd scream in the night. I'd hide under the bedcovers, waiting and listening. I still hide and wait and listen. Afraid of the angry explosion I won't see coming, but I know will be my fault.

# CHARACTER TEMPLATE

## STRANGER TO HER HEART

**Physical Info:**
Slim, athletic woman aged 45. She is 5'5" and has long blonde wavy hair. Her skin is weathered and wrinkled around her eyes. She has Crohn's disease and has a stoma.

**Expositional Facts:**
Raised in the Outer Hebrides Islands, off the West Coast of Scotland. She moved to Glasgow to get a job when she finished school. Studied Environmental Science in university. She has a female partner, two border terriers, and no children.

**Occupation:**
Used to work for Intrepid, leading expeditions and hikes all over the world. Ten years ago, she joined "Octopus", a green energy company, she is a field engineer.

**Habits:**
Drives a green Volkswagen Beetle when she isn't in her camper van. She loves reading magazines like Climber and National Geographic. She lives in overalls and outdoor work gear.

**Hobbies:**
Travels all over Europe in her camper van. Loves rock climbing and climbs every weekend in the mountains. She is also a mountain leader and takes groups up mountains. She just likes to be outside as much as possible.

**Phobias:**
Claustrophobia – fear of small spaces. Doesn't like crowds or cities.

**Temperament:**
Confident and very assertive. Has a positive outlook on life and always a glass more than half full.

**Traumas/Unusual Compulsions:**
Her father died when she was five and her mother, finding it hard to cope, became an alcoholic. She has a fear of abandonment as she was abandoned by both parents. She had to be the parent to her siblings.

**Food Preferences:**
Vegetarian, gluten, and dairy-free. She is allergic to nuts and shellfish. Her diet is limited because of the Crohn's disease.

**What is in their fridge/medicine cabinet:**
Fridge: Oat milk, coconut yogurt, 5 bottles of kefir, tofu, spinach, 5 eggs, blueberries, probiotics, 2 bowls of raw meat for the dogs.
Medicine cabinet: Prednisolone, tea tree oil, Bazuka, duct tape, sun cream, a packet of 10 tampons, baby oil, wet wipes, and a box of colostomy bags.

*Margo George*

# STRANGER TO HER HEART
## BY MARGO GEORGE

Despite Jesse's lifelong battle with health, her glass was always half full. She grew up in the Outer Hebrides, on a remote island with a population of a hundred people, sixty kilometres west of Scotland. There were four children in her class at school, her younger sister being one of them.

Her dad died when she was five and her mother turned to alcohol to anaesthetize her pain. She spent much of her time alone with her best friend, a border terrier called Fionn. They explored caves together and took out a small boat around the island. She got little attention from anyone and looked out for herself. A daily grind, she did a two-hour shift on the community allotment, which they relied on for fresh vegetables and fruit.

In the night Jesse would often be doubled over in pain. She didn't get to the bottom of it until she moved to Glasgow on the mainland, at eighteen.

The pain continued to crush her insides and rob her of energy. One day the pain was so great she went to A&E (Accident and Emergency) in Glasgow. After a lot of tests, she got diagnosed with Crohn's disease. Her bowel was damaged beyond repair.

There was no choice of treatment. The surgeon removed a large section of her bowel, which left her intestines exiting her abdomen, and an ostomy bag to collect her poo. This disability had a huge impact on her life.

Her only visitors in the hospital Intensive Care Unit when she woke up, were her two friends.

"I called your mum," one friend said.

"I told you not to," Jesse said.

She felt her friend's concern. She could not let her disability beat her. She overcame the adjustments she had to make to her life, one at a time.

She landed a job, doing field work with a Green Energy Company. She tied her unbrushed hair up, donned her blue overalls, her steel-toe-capped boots and drove to work each day in her green Volkswagen Beetle. She was outside, getting dirty and making an impact.

She never returned to the Outer Hebrides and has not seen her mum or sister since she left. Inside her mind lurks the pain of abandonment and loneliness. Tough and independent on the outside, her focus is survival. Inside, Jesse is a stranger to her heart.

# CHARACTER TEMPLATE

## SCARS

**Physical Info:**

African-American woman, a large afro twice the size of her face. Medium/tall (5'9"), large, upturned nose. She has long angular fingers, thin legs, and is medium build.

**Expositional Facts:**

Raised in Philadelphia and went to Temple University. Major in Fashion, minor in accounting. Middle daughter, older sister, and younger brother. She is divorced from an abusive husband. She has a tattoo on her back shoulder and a scar on her buttocks from being beaten by her ex. She has a recurring dream of being a lion tamer. Clothes vary from Boho ethnic chick to accounting blah.

**Occupation:**

Works as an accountant for a TV show. She had started out as a retail stylist and for a while worked in the wardrobe closet for a movie.

**Habits:**

OCD, checks watch every 30 minutes. When she is in public, she looks over her shoulder every few minutes. Is obsessed with cleanliness and orderliness and wipes all the surfaces of her kitchen 2-3 times a day. She has crisp $100 bills in a hidden compartment of her wallet. She counts the money three times a day.

**Hobbies:**
Macramé, sewing ethnic style jackets, collecting stamps, and her cat.

**Phobias:**
Chronophobia – fear of time or time passing. Fearful and jumpy all the time, particularly with loud noises.

**Temperament:**
Serious and always worrying.

**Traumas/Unusual Compulsions:**
Father was stabbed to death when she was five years old. She was in the house when it happened, and she heard her father begging for his life. Her ex was abusive.

**Food Preferences:**
Tries to be a vegan but is a closet carnivore. She is allergic to carrots.

**What is in their fridge/medicine cabinet:**
Fridge: coffee, pastrami, hot mustard, collard greens, Thousand Island dressing.
Medicine cabinet: Valium, caffeine pills, Trazadone.
Glove Compartment: cowbell, whistle, mini massager, Band-Aids, condoms.

*Tsilah Burman*

# SCARS

## BY TSILAH BURMAN

Norma was at a vegan restaurant with two work colleagues, to celebrate the closing of the quarter one books, for the television show *The Gentlemen*. Norma was dark-skinned with an afro twice the size of her face. She had a beauty etched with angular features and a seriousness in her demeanor. She tried being vegan, but loved her meat—crisp bacon, her favorite. Norma liked the orderliness of accounting—different from her stints as a retail stylist and working the wardrobe closet for a movie that never made it to the screen. Another failure, like her marriage. She was beaten by her husband for three years, until her brother whisked her away to a safe house.

As a child, she spent the first five years of her life in Los Angeles where her parents were entrenched in the Black Panther movement, particularly her father. She'd been plagued with guilt since the day she pretended to be sick, so she could spend some one-on-one time with her dad.

"You were supposed to take him down, and you didn't," the man said to her father. Norma was in the bedroom she shared with her older sister and younger brother, who were at the makeshift Panther school. The family was cramped in a two-bedroom rental in Watts. Bars were on the windows of the tiny house. A bitten off fingernail lay on the floor next to two mattresses along with picture books, paper and crayons. "Don't!" her dad said. Norma heard a slashing sound, a scream, a large thump on the floor and a door slammed shut. She heard her dad whimpering, telling her to stay in her room. And then it was silent.

Two hours later, her mother found her father stabbed to death, caked in blood, and Norma cowering in the corner of her bedroom. Three months later, Norma's mom left the movement, packed up their meagre belongings and relocated her family to Philadelphia. Norma got a degree from Temple University in fashion and accounting. In her mid-twenties, she was diagnosed with PTSD and OCD. She was obsessed with time, checking her watch and looking over her shoulder every five minutes. She still jumps when she hears loud noises.

# CHARACTER TEMPLATE
## RING FINGER

**Physical Info:**

Slim, athletic woman, late 30s, 5'9" ish, bleach blonde frizzy hair in a bun. Wears immaculate navy skirt suits with white open-collared shirts. Has manicured nails and carries a leather briefcase.

**Expositional Facts:**

Raised in Devon, UK. Lower middle-class family. Close to her mother, resents her father. Divorced but was married when younger. No children but wishes she did have. A-type personality. Excelled in school and work.

**Occupation:**

Humanitarian lawyer at a prestigious law firm. Six-figure salary.

**Habits:**

Ex-smoker likes to drink expensive alcohol and cocktails e.g. Grey Goose, champagne, and martinis. Often touches her hair to make sure it's in place.

**Hobbies:**

Long distance running, peloton, reading self-help books on relationships and parenthood.

**Phobias:**

Mageirocophobia—fear of cooking. She always eats out or has restaurant food delivered once or twice a day.

**Temperament:**
Hard-working, manically driven, ambitious, assertive to the point that at times she is blunt and insensitive. She uses this to disarm her clients and her colleagues.

**Traumas/Unusual Compulsions:**
She had an abusive stepfather who beat her mother. This led to chronic anxiety which she deals with by overworking, alcohol, and online dating. She doesn't see the same man twice. Often speaks her thoughts out loud to strangers on the street.

**Food Preferences:**
Obsessive about health. She is a flexitarian with a penchant for rare steak and fresh oysters.

**What is in her refrigerator/medicine cabinet:**
Fridge: Oat milk, coconut water, bottled VOSS water, Sancerre white wine, mustard, and mayonnaise. Her freezer contains ice and vodka.
Medicine cabinet: Xanax, sleeping pills, and three containers of codeine. Birth control pills.

*Bianca Bazin*

# RING FINGER
## BY BIANCA BAZIN

Sophie swayed in a haze among twirling blossom leaves, slouched on a slatted wooden bench in the park nearest her three-bed Edwardian semi in Southwest London. Her long, slender legs were splayed across the seat, while she muttered beneath her breath, clutching the remnants of a bottle of Grey Goose vodka in her right hand. Her frizzy blonde hair, riled by the wind, and her flushed complexion unnerved the dog walkers, despite her immaculate navy-blue suit and fine leather briefcase nestled beneath the seat. If a naïve stranger wandered too close, Sophie would bark, "Justice? You're a fucking fool."

The alcohol numbed the throbbing of the scar on Sophie's belly from an emergency C-section four years ago. Sophie survived, her baby and her marriage did not. She sat staring ahead, stroking the indent on her ring finger that remained carved there, despite the years it had lain bare. A graveyard of cigarette butts lay scattered around Sophie's feet—a vice she had quit at the tail end of her teens and resurrected due to the mounting pressure of defending the rights of those who had been silenced, wronged and torn.

Today she was meant to be defending a rape victim, arguing for the termination of their pregnancy at twenty-four weeks.

She called in sick as she exited the off-licence this morning. Her associate went instead.

Sophie chose humanitarian law, believing she could right the wrongs from her childhood. Determined and tough, she made partner at thirty-five. After each case she won, she travelled back to what remained of her scorched, boarded-up house near the moors where she lost her mum, to remind her of the justice she was fighting for. After the loss of her baby, each victory became an increasing rattle, jangling in her hollow chest, the way her stepfather's keys did that night as he fumbled to open the front door, a bottle of Jack down and a simmering fuse, while the scent of the bubbling Bolognese on the fire stove oozed up the stairs and into Sophie's bedroom. As she sat on the bench, Sophie's gold and blue eyes glistened like a winter morning's dew, consumed in the kind of memory and grief only vodka could subdue.

# CHARACTER TEMPLATE

## THE DESIGNER

**Physical Info:**
Late 20s, short, slim, pretty, long dark hair with a fringe. She is shortsighted but doesn't wear glasses. Likes to wear makeup and always has purple fingernails.

**Expositional Facts:**
She is an only child and went to a strict Catholic girls' school. Has had one long relationship that has just ended. She had a very loving but intensely strict father who over-managed her.

**Occupation:**
Working at present in a café but has worked in the fashion industry.

**Habits:**
She makes a point of eating at a snail's pace. She says it's because she wants to savour her food. Others think it's a control thing. She drives a MINI Cooper and drives it fast.

**Hobbies:**
Makes her own clothes, she loves the colour blue, she collects glass angels, and has them on most of the surfaces at home.

**Phobias:**
Angrophobia, fear of conflict, and she has conflict anxiety.

**Temperament:**
Playful and outgoing when she gets to know people. Shy and controlled on the surface.

**Traumas/Unusual Compulsions:**
Makes lists every morning of what she needs to do. Everything she does is listed from cleaning her teeth, going to the bathroom, what she ate, and what time. She lists what she will wear the next days, clothes, shoes, and accessories. At night she checks everything off.

**Food Preferences:**
Vegan but likes cheese and if it's on the list, and once a week it is, she will have cheese made with cow's milk.

**What is in their fridge/medicine cabinet:**
Fridge: One bottle of white wine, cheese hidden under mounds of green vegetables. On the fridge door is a list to keep a record of what she needs to buy.
Medicine cabinet: Packets of antacids and Xanax are hidden in the back behind bottles of homeopathic pills and some Chinese potions. A small glass angel.

*Christine Mander*

# THE DESIGNER
## BY CHRISTINE MANDER

She sat in the corner of the cafe, nearest the coffee bar, eating her lunch. Each bite was considered. She was slim and pretty with long dark hair and a fringe. Her makeup was neat, her nails were dark purple. She had that vague look that goes with being short-sighted but wasn't wearing any glasses.

I realised she worked there when a customer arrived at the till. She leapt up and headed behind the counter leaving her half-eaten lunch on the table. She was shorter than I'd imagined and wore a black skirt with a top that had one side longer than the other, with buckles placed from the shoulder across to the opposite side. It was made from a mixture of materials with mismatched colours and textures. Fabrics I would never have dreamt of mixing but that worked well together. Her tights were maroon, and she was wearing black pixie boots with silver buckles. She chatted with the customer but seemed shy.

On subsequent visits to the café, I discovered she was only working there until she could get her fashion business off the ground. She had just come out of a long relationship. She had done everything for the guy, washing his clothes, cooking his meals and cleaning the small flat they shared. It was her way of showing love, but she'd expected him to look after her in return. He thought she enjoyed doing those things, she always told him she did, and so he was surprised when she left him. She packed up her collection of glass angels and took off in the MINI Cooper her father had bought for her. She was an only child, sent to a Catholic school where she had learnt you need to take care of your man. Her father's strict ways hadn't disabused her of this belief. Something she was reassessing for her next relationship. It'll be a while though, as she takes time to lose her shyness with new people. The new man needs to be a vegan, but maybe this time she'll tell him she still likes a bit of real cheese, when she's not out with her vegan friends.

# CHARACTER TEMPLATE
## DEATH BY OLEANDER

**Physical Info:**

Manicured nails, 170 cm tall. About 30. 20:20 vision, cornflower blue eyes. Olympian 5-ring tattoo on left upper arm. Facial wart on left side of nose. Never wears makeup. Shoulder-length brown hair, thin brown eyebrows.

**Expositional Facts:**

Grew up in Stockholm. Only child. Mother died of breast cancer when she was 10. Father worked in the oil industry. He was away for 3 months at a time, home for 6. He is now in jail after being the 'fall guy' for a BP oil spill. She speaks five languages and is pansexual.

**Occupation:**

Executive chef at a 9-bed chalet in Swiss Alps. Off-season is an event chef in the Caribbean. Trained at Leiths in London and spent 2 years at a Michelin 3-star restaurant in Italy.

**Habits:**

Chews the ends of her hair. Cracks her knuckles as she cooks. Walks with a strut like a supermodel on a catwalk. Loves riding a Honda 650 motorcycle.

**Hobbies:**

Ski off-piste. Olympic silver medallist in sharpshooting. Watches French movies, collects butterflies, grows edible flowers, and dreams of being a Master of Wine. Experiments with poisonous flowers and plants like hemlock and oleander.

**Phobias:**

Chiroptophobia—fear of bats. Thalassophobia—fear of drowning.

**Temperament:**

Focused. Perfectionism. Presents food with showmanship style. She is shrewd, empathetic, listens well. Is flirty. Likes to make people feel relaxed and happy.

**Traumas/Unusual Compulsions:**

Abandonment issues from mother and father. Has nightmares about when her dad was taken to jail. Has sex with strangers and with the married men and women who come to the lodge.

**Food Preferences:**

Favourite meal is lobster. Loves homemade ice cream. Drinks Perrier and champagne while cooking. Eggs with smoked salmon or caviar for breakfast.

**What is in their fridge/medicine cabinet:**

Fridge: French cheeses. Greek Yogurt. Pinot Noir mustard. Black and white truffles. Jars of pickles. A bottle of insulin. Medicine cabinet: Sleeping pills, a bottle of NAD+, a tube of anal lube, insulin syringes, a box of anti-depressants, a box of condoms, and powdered oleander.

*Fiona Jacob*

# DEATH BY OLEANDER

## BY FIONA JACOB

Lotta bowed over the cheese soufflé appetizers, she'd just removed from the oven. She held her breath. Her timing was perfect. The soufflés had risen up from the white Villeroy & Boch ramekins and were light and airy. She smiled as the pungent nutty smells of aged Parmigiano-Reggiano and Gruyère wafted across the large stainless-steel kitchen.

She could hear animated conversations, interspersed with laughter, and the chink of champagne glasses in the dining room. The group of twelve skiers, included the board of British Petroleum, the same company her father worked for before he landed in jail over an oil spill, and their partners. They'd already opened four bottles of 2012 Louis Roederer Cristal to celebrate their final night at The Lodge.

Tonight would be a food triumph, Lotta mused. She had created a memorable five course menu with twice-baked cheese soufflés, assiette of rabbit, marinated spatchcock quail and almond panna cotta and apricot sorbet, raspberries, hibiscus meringue. Of course, there was a perfect wine pairing to match each dish.

Lotta wore full chef's whites and a tall, pleated chef's toque. The stark white was in contrast to her dark brown hair, pulled off her face into a tight ponytail. She wore no make-up except for a dab of pink lip gloss that made her cornflower blue eyes pop.

As usual, before she began plating, she cracked her knuckles. Wearing blue latex gloves, and using forceps, she placed purple flowering broccoli, then added violets, oleander and yellow pumpkin flowers, followed by shavings of black truffle and hazelnut oil. Each dish looked like a Monet painting.

"Careful," Lotta said to Adrianna, the South African server. From the dining room, she could hear the roars of approval as the appetizers were served, followed by the glug of red wine being poured into balloon wine glasses.

Lotta sighed.

Her eyes rested on the stainless-steel table where the handmade chocolates she had tempered earlier in the day, lay in perfect rows. These delicacies, decadent butterfly chocolates tasted of burnt caramel and Piedmont hazelnut, tarragon grapefruit, and her own favourite, sesame nougat.

She decided that later she would place the chocolates in a matt black box, with a black and cream velvet ribbon, and then give each guest these as a parting gift, a memento of their time together in Verbier.

She would not tell them about oleander.

Oh, revenge was sweet.

# CHARACTER TEMPLATE

## MAKE LEMONADE WHEN LIFE GIVES YOU LEMONS

**Physical Info:**
Short, 5'3". Flabby stomach, shiny bald head, multifocal glasses. Always dressed immaculately.

**Expositional Facts:**
Raised on a dairy farm. Is happily married but has no kids. Was bullied at school and by his brothers for being so different.

**Occupation:**
Unemployed, lives off inheritance. Used to work in a local bakery on and off but was sacked for eating too many cakes.

**Habits:**
Has nails manicured every week. Showers twice a day. Could have a full head of hair but likes to shave it daily himself.

**Hobbies:**
Makes miniature models of fast cars, loves the details, the painting, and putting them together. Also, owns and drives fast cars.

**Phobias:**
Mysophobia, verminophobia and bacillophobia. Fastidious about cleanliness. Wipes kitchen surfaces multiple times a day. Polishes all shoes and his glasses every night.

**Temperament:**
Lively, fun-loving, vengeful.

**Traumas/Unusual Compulsions:**
Has a full-blown PTSD breakdown if he smells cow dung. His brothers threw him into a cow dung pile as a kid.

**Food Preferences:**
Loves anything sweet. Chocolate, cakes, all desserts, and ice cream. Has to eat ice cream after every meal including breakfast.

**What is in their fridge/medicine cabinet:**
Fridge: Steak, fresh cream cakes, 17 dark and milk chocolate bars. Beer.
Medicine cabinet: Fire lighter, paraffin oil, candles, matches, sleeping pills.
A yellow-stained envelope that says 'My Revenge List' on the outside.

*Hilda Rhodes*

# MAKE LEMONADE WHEN LIFE GIVES YOU LEMONS

## BY HILDA RHODES

I admired my reflection in the long mirror. My skin felt and looked clean. I'd taken an extra-long shower this morning, because my body was sticky and hot from lovemaking with Mona. She is the love of my life, and she loves me, despite my weird habits. I have to shower twice every day. A sad thought flitted across my brain—we can't have kids. I switched to visualising driving my E-type Jaguar. I love that car. We are both short and cuddly, so it's a bit of a squeeze getting in and out, but it's so much fun.

I surveyed my clothes. A tight fawn cashmere sweater topped pale blue hipster denims. Shiny black pointed boots with Cuban heels complete my outfit. My bald head gleamed. The lenses of my multi focal gold-rimmed glasses were clear and spotless. My gold wedding band on my ring finger was tight, but my manicured nails looked great.

Thoughts drifted to my childhood. Growing up on a dairy farm, the youngest of five boys had been hard. No chance then of having manicured nails! My older brothers took after my father, strong and muscular. I was soft and flabby. My brothers' idea of fun was to push me into the dung heap and laugh. No amount of scrubbing got rid of the stink of cow shit from my skin. My mother didn't say much. She didn't want to upset my father. He had a violent temper.

School had been a bullying nightmare too; first of all, Maffra Primary, then Maffra Secondary College. My nickname was Piggy. I was hopeless at sports. I struggled to read and write, but I loved fast car magazines. I saved my pocket money to buy miniature model sports cars. Time and suffering disappeared when I was painting and putting the tiny parts together.

I met Mona at the bakery where I worked after leaving school. I was sacked for eating too many cakes. My parents kicked me out, so I moved in with Mona. Then the tragedy happened. I felt my penis harden as I recalled the headline—*Family Killed by Mysterious Fire at Local Farm.*

I sold the farm for three million dollars, bought my E-type and invested the remainder. My motto: make lemonade when life gives you lemons.

# CHARACTER TEMPLATE
## *FASCISM NEVER SLEEPS*

**Physical Info:**
82-year-old woman. Uses a 4-pronged cane. Was once a lean, sinewy ballerina but is now plump, hunched, and arthritic. Wears a brown wig.

**Expositional Facts:**
She was born in Bucharest, Romania. Father was a doctor, mother a music teacher. She has an older brother and a younger sister. She was smuggled out of Romania in a turnip truck through Yugoslavia to Greece. Later emigrated to the USA.

**Occupation:**
Full-time prima ballerina throughout the world. Later taught ballet.

**Habits:**
She is a loner and prefers her own company. Is interested in politics and watches all the news shows including Al Jazeera. She soaks her worn-out feet in warm milk.

**Hobbies:**
She loves cooking, particularly Romanian dishes. She collects recipes on 5 x 3 colored notecards filed by country. She collects ballet slippers that she buys on eBay.

**Phobias:**
Eisoptrophobia—fear of mirrors.

**Temperament:**
Was once very lively, energetic, and hopeful. Now she is blunted by loss and trauma.

**Traumas/Unusual Compulsions:**
Prone to flashbacks and anxiety from the atrocities she witnessed in Bucharest. Has a deep-rooted fear of authority or autocracy.

**Food Preferences:**
Romanian Sarmale and Stufat. Polenta, Sweetbreads, and all sorts of sausage. She doesn't eat vegetables at all except for sweet potatoes.

**What is in their fridge/medicine cabinet:**
Fridge: Virsli, Pleșcoi, and Offal sausages. Bottle of Țuică. Heinz ketchup. Saucer with diamond rings. 80% dark chocolate. One egg and a can of coke.

Medicine cabinet: Valium, oxycodone, fentanyl. Scalp/wig glue, and a gold picture frame with a picture of her as a young ballerina.

*Mary White*

# FASCISM NEVER SLEEPS

## BY MARY WHITE

Alone on her birthday, Elena settles into her wingback chair reading the *New York Times*. She sips Cognac and relishes the quiet in her Brooklyn apartment. Aromas of pork sausage, polenta and sweet bread waft from the kitchen. An article detailing a presidential candidate's insidious rhetoric makes her skin crawl. The self-obsessed pandering sounds familiar to her.

With the help of a four-pronged cane, Elena stands up and shuffles toward a chest full of memorabilia. Catching her reflection in a mirror, she shudders and looks away. Her once smooth porcelain skin is withered and saggy. A short brown wig replaces long, shiny black hair. Her former lean, sinewy ballerina body is plump, hunched and arthritic.

She opens the chest, takes out a faded photo of her parents and falls into a reverie of a happy childhood in Bucharest. Born to a physician father and music teacher mother, she was the middle child between a mischievous older brother and an adoring younger sister. In the early years, their home life was easy, warm and plentiful. Elena's parents supported her ballet career as she had obvious talent. Over time, their happy life was shadowed by a burgeoning cloud of despair under the rule of President Ceaușescu, a self-aggrandizing autocrat whose austere policies caused mass starvation, disease and other atrocities.

As a young adult, Elena attended a resistance meeting that was raided by the president's police. She escaped but was recognized by an officer who knew her father. To avoid imprisonment, she was smuggled out of the country in the back of a turnip truck through Yugoslavia. From there she traveled to the home of a cousin in Greece.

Tragedy persisted in Romania. One by one, she lost her beloved family and friends to incarceration or illness. Despite the trauma she endured, Elena maintained her ballet practice and career. Dance was her refuge, her escape, her sanity. In time, she emigrated to New York and began teaching.

Elena returns to her chair and ponders the current threat to freedom posed by self-serving, power-hungry wannabe leaders who rely on personality, over sound, equitable policy. Ever hopeful that democracy will reign in this country, she vows to stay aware and informed. For, as a friend once told her, "Fascism never sleeps."

# PART IV

# 75% LIES

The invitation or suggestion of Jack's "Creating and Building a Fictional Character," class is, if you are doing the steps in this book, do the weeks in sequential order. Week four, 75% lies, will be more interesting and fun once the writer has explored creating a Character Template and taking themselves on a Character Date.

Each of the pieces in this next chapter are at least 75% lies. It will be fun for you, to decide what you think might be a lie. It is often not the obvious that are lies. It's the little things that are more subtle that tend to hold lies within them. Don't be too quick to see what you think are the lies. But hey 75%, yep, is a lot of lies.

> *Once you pass about 50% made-up-material, you might as well be at 100% because it's almost impossible to do 100% given the fact that no matter how much we invent or imagine, so much of what we write is informed by our own emotional experience.*
>
> — Jack Grapes

There is fact in all fiction, and fiction in all fact. However much we think we can remember exactly what has happened in our lives, we make things up. We make things up when we are telling someone a story and we even make things up in our memories.

What is really 'true' when you describe your personal history? If you were to ask my two sisters and me to recount the events around our father's drinking, you'd find two of us declare that our father was indeed an alcoholic, and a third sister *"What do you mean Dad was a drinker?"* We can only ever write our own reality and at times use fiction to create the same feeling we had in the moment. Even the sister and I, who knew our father was an alcoholic, still experienced and would write the events differently.

With that in mind it is suggested that the writer find their deep voice, the feeling of a particular experience, and then they lie to their heart's content all over the page.

Maybe you describe your wedding but instead of the bride, you were the bridesmaid, wishing the bride would do a runner, as she told you the night before, she was going to. And you, thrilled at this news, because you've been having an affair with the groom for a year. Betrayal. Then you share more lies about the day and come up for truth air, and then more lies.

With 75% lies, you can do one piece where they write about just one particular experience and dig into it. And then, on another day, write a piece with a bunch of different experiences and see what that reveals to you. Not different stories but different experiences of the same story.

Play a little and misplace yourself as you take on the persona of the liar. Come on, that must sound like a bit of fun!

# CULCHIE
## BY MARGO GEORGE

I was ten when I lived on a farm in Ireland, two miles from a village with a church, five pubs and a shop. Mammy was devoid of emotion. Daddy a true Irish gent, wedded to his social rank. I heard him sob every night. Mammy consoled him. I came down for breakfast, to the sizzle of fried eggs, rashers, sausages, and black pudding. Daddy always sat next to the stove. He took me onto his knee and bounced me up and down. He laughed, but his eyes were sad. My two younger brothers, dull and ambitionless, were blotted out by me.

It was the Easter Holidays, and in two weeks I was to return to boarding school sixty miles away. This was my second visit home since I started in September. From one hellhole to the next. At school I was a hillbilly surrounded by posh kids. Nobody wanted to know me, except to laugh at my hideous hand-me-down clothes and my culchie ways. All out of sorts, I was not like the others. I cried myself to sleep at night. I got respite in drama class, where I pretended I was someone else, someone better, someone popular, someone intelligent, someone loved. I counted down the days to when I'd be old enough to quit the life that devoured my soul. I begged Mother Mary and baby Jesus in my prayers to rescue me. Pleas that went unheeded.

Every night I wrote down my dreams in a brown leather embossed journal I got from mammy when she dropped me off at this hideous place the first time. I would live in a big house that I would paint in bright colours, furnish with antiques and lavish silk curtains. I will have a husband who would love me and at least ten kids. I won't have a lonely child, with no friends and a family that couldn't care two figs about her. I will entertain, be a socialite, go to the dances and travel the world. I would wear posh frocks, dainty shoes, patent handbags in all the colours, delicate shawls, and brooches encrusted with precious stones. My dreams assumed my reality, and this was how I made it out alive.

# ALLIE AND ME
## BY KRYSTEEN DVORACEK

"You're our first Associate to get pregnant," said Des, my boss. "I suppose you'll be wanting to take the full twelve months maternity leave?" We were standing in his corner office on the 23rd floor of 101 Collins Street, in the heart of Melbourne's business district. My rounded belly was barely noticeable in my grey tailored suit. A perfect string of white pearls stretched high against my bare neck.

"No need," I said. "We've already lined up our nanny to start after three weeks." Jack, my husband, and I had agreed a baby wouldn't derail my career. A perfect power couple, soon to be power parents, with a perfect twenty-year plan. We'd selected the best private school for this little one and the one in the freezer to follow. I'd booked my C-section to line up post the big corporate merger I was working on. I had an Excel spreadsheet for my nursery purchases and the pantry stacked for after the birth.

None of which prepared me for what happened. How tidal waves of contractions hit and almost sunk me, until I grunted and swayed letting my body find its rhythm. How I delivered, kneeling on all fours, panting like a dog. How I pulled my baby to my naked breast and inhaled her scent and fine blond hair.

How much I loved her sucking at my breasts, stirring a love that surpassed anything I felt for Jack.

I found myself at war with Jack. He banged on about all those years I'd spent at law school – why had I bothered, if I was just going to stay home? That we'd bought our two-storey home on a two-income mortgage and little Allie deserved a good school. But what if Allie was sick? Not seriously sick, just sick enough to give me a reason to stay home with her.

I couldn't shake the idea out of my mind. It took root as I rocked her during our 4 a.m. feeds. Allie in my arms and my laptop perched, as Dr Google and I hatched our plan. It wasn't fair for us to be separated. This way we wouldn't be. No one would dare get between me and my sick baby girl. Allie and me.

# I'LL HUNT THEM DOWN
## BY TSILAH BURMAN

Men shattered the hearts of the women in my family.

My father abandoned my mother and me when I was five.

At the age of ten, my mother and I were at the Farmer's Market for lunch and shopping. As we strolled to the toy store, a gold Cadillac drove by. A bald man wearing a fedora was at the wheel. A man with a red moustache sat atop the back seat waving a shotgun. He took aim and fired at the first person who caught his eye—my mother. I dropped to the ground, laid on top of her and begged her to breathe. But she was gone. Tears tsunami'd me, as parts of my soul died with her.

Abandoned, I went to live with my grandmother, a proud Lithuanian-born woman, who built tile floors in Israel in the late 1920s and twenty years later in America, fended for herself and her two daughters when her husband died at the age of forty-two.

As a detective, my motive is to search for men to hang them up to dry. I've been responsible for forty-eight blokes being locked up. When I'm put on a case, guys tremble, as they should.

But I've failed. I couldn't solve my mother's case, or the case of a dismembered woman in L.A. left in a gutter on skid row. A Council member's sapphire tie coiled around her severed neck. A local optometrist's psychedelic jock strap encircled the lone pelvis, separated from its core.

The Council member, a debonair, 5'10" athlete turned politician, had three young children in diapers and a trophy wife. Slick as steel, but distraught at the interrogation. He claimed he had necrophobia, so couldn't have committed the murder. He'd flirted with the deceased at a Hollywood strip club two days before the body was found.

The eye doctor, a nebbish of medium build with a paunch, wore prism glasses. An anonymous tip said his wife was frigid, and he spent his evenings at porn houses on Hollywood Boulevard, where he paid to have sex with the deceased three days before the incident.

Both suspects disappeared and could not be traced, like my father, and my mother's killer.

I'll hunt them down.

# AN OPEN WINDOW
## BY HILDA RHODES

Despair flooded my whole being. My baby's wailing twanged on my sensitive nerves. I shrieked for her to stop. She didn't. Hot tears blurred my vision as I looked down at this tiny bundle of pink flesh with its eyes screwed shut and its mouth wide open.

I'd never wanted a baby. I was fourteen when my elder sister caught TB. My mum, a bitter widow from WWI, made me take care of her. The ungrateful bitch never appreciated what I gave up for her. She was allowed to stay on at school until she was sixteen, but I'd had to leave at thirteen. I got a job with the Royal Insurance. Promotions were scarce for a girl who'd left school at thirteen. I got married during WWII to get away from the two of them. Finding this small room and kitchen in the West End of Glasgow was a stroke of luck.

WWII was a godsend for me. Career opportunities for women opened up. My mind flew back to when I had a proper job, a paid job, to when I had my own money. Getting up in the morning to go to work had been so easy. Each morning, I would admire my reflection in the long wardrobe door mirror; the fitted wool coat, the smart black high-heeled shoes with matching handbag, my felt hat perched on my head at a jaunty angle. I'd felt like the bee's knees.

## An Open Window

The war ended. My husband came home. His dream was a quiet life. I was supposed to stay at home, look after the children and have a meal ready when he came home from work. My position at work had been given to a returned serviceman. I felt trapped. I needed a way out!

The front door crashing open shattered my despair fuelled imagination.

"Mary, give her to me," she said. Mrs Forsyth, the old lady who lived downstairs, stood between me and the open window. My spare door key lay on the floor. Her blue eyes were wide open, her breathing laboured, her chest heaved. She took my screaming baby from my outstretched arms. I slumped into a chair. I hadn't killed her. Not yet.

# MOTHER KNOWS BEST
## BY BIANCA BAZIN

I was born on my due date; July 10th, 1991. It was a Wednesday. However, as my mother ballooned in the preceding months, she decided that, like my brother, I was to arrive late and so, since mothers know best, she'd take a trip up north to visit her friend, Imogen, instead of packing a hospital bag. She booked herself a first-class ticket on the 9 am train from London to Newcastle on July 10th. It would take six hours, and the peace would allow her time to finish her novel.

"Is this a good idea, love?" my father asked. "What if she comes on time?"

My mother stared into his pleading eyes. His usual pale complexion was flushed, and his black hair appeared static, like he'd stuck his finger into a socket.

"I know my daughter, and no, she's not coming tomorrow," my mother said with a smug smile while she rubbed her belly. I kicked back.

So, there we were, shuttling towards Newcastle, my mother in a floaty red dress surrounded by important men in black suits. I waited until the train departed Cambridge, and then promptly pressed the eject button. Twenty-five minutes later, my mother was squatting on the train floor over a pile of donated suit jackets.

A few screams later, with the train guard at the helm, I arrived atop of the pile. I was blue and not breathing, strangled by my mother's determination to know best, to keep me in. The train guard called out into the crowd of gawping men, "Does anyone know infant CPR?" turns out spreadsheets don't prepare one for the menial task of childbirth. The response came in the form of a tiny "Achoo!" from the baby in his arms. I took my first breath and cried. The train guard returned me to my mother who smiled and asked for a pair of scissors.

At 3.30 pm, my mother rung Imogen's doorbell. Grinning from ear to ear, with me in her arms wrapped in a bloody scarf she said, "This one's going to keep me on my toes." Then she pushed her way through the post-box red front door, thrust me into Imogen's arms and collapsed in the hall.

# LUCKIEST, HAPPIEST PEOPLE IN THE WORLD

## BY MARY WHITE

I grew up in a fairy tale. I was the youngest of three by eleven and fifteen years. We lived in a mansion in Minneapolis. My father was a litigation lawyer and well-liked State Representative. Warm, clever and astute at reading a room, he was a natural politician and irresistible to his fans. My mother was quiet, deep and never missed a nuance. We were a close, fun, loving family.

I have vivid memories of the parties my parents threw, especially during campaign season when the neighborhood was speckled with black and orange lawn signs for Richard White. I came alive at the parties as I impressed the well-dressed, good smelling guests with my proficient vocabulary, clever turns of phrase and firm handshake at age eight. I mingled with Representatives, Senators, directors, chairs and their spouses. While they were dazzled by my precociousness, I was mesmerized by the tailored suits, colorful cocktail dresses, gem-laden jewelry and how light beams danced off the crystal champagne glasses.

Sometimes, I performed classical piano pieces, Chopin Preludes or Bach Inventions. But my father was the true entertainer.

Everyone gathered around the old upright, singing, as his hands glided over the ivories. We were the luckiest, happiest people in the world.

In the fall of 1971, my sister Anne went missing. She was an effervescent twenty-three-year-old artist who lived in an apartment downtown. When the ransom note arrived, my father slumped in his chair and cried. Early in his career as a litigator, he'd prosecuted a mobster from St. Paul and put him away for racketeering, money laundering and manslaughter. His son wanted revenge and kidnapped Anne at a premium price.

Our once happy, free-spirited home became hushed and stoic. Muffled voices and squelched cries emanated from behind closed doors. My brother came home from college grim faced and sullen. A heavy melancholy hung in the air and the gaiety was replaced with a dour seriousness. When at last my sister was released everyone was overjoyed, but the color of our lives faded. My father sank into depression and the bottle. He lost the next election. He lost our home. He lost his will to live. I needed a miracle.

# INHERITANCE
## BY CHRISTINE MANDER

I'm sitting in the kitchen. It's almost lunch time. It's a wet, cold day and I don't have to go out. I'm halfway through a jigsaw on the table. I find it calms me down and I love the feeling of elation when a piece fits. I like finding pieces that fit. I've spent a lifetime feeling like I don't fit.

The wrong person in the wrong place. I'm adopted and I never felt like I belonged in my family. My parents, the ones who adopted me, are academic and intelligent. The most important thing for them is to be able to use your brain. To juggle lots of competing ideas and synthesise the truth from them. Or a truth I should say. In their minds, your body is just something to carry your brains around.

I loved movement and I loved dance. I loved acting and I loved creating things from nothing. They didn't understand this part of me. They were always telling me to sit still, to pick up a book, to revise for my exams. Movement seemed alien to them. It unnerved them; they said they couldn't think when I was rushing round the house or playing music.

They are very well known, of course, and were always being asked to speak on the radio or at conferences. They did their research together, so they had their own language. Words that made sense to them but left me feeling excluded. At the beginning they tried to include me, to encourage me to be like them, but my brain just didn't work in the same way. I could tell they were disappointed, they'd wanted someone to carry on their work, to create a dynasty but that was never going to happen.

Eventually I escaped and went to drama school. At first, they tried to keep in touch, but they were too busy, too much in demand. They didn't understand what I was doing, why I would want to pretend to be other people. Why I would want to create something unique of my own. I felt sorry for them. I'd disappointed them, but I couldn't be what they wanted me to be. It just wasn't possible.

# BUTTERCUPS
## BY TRISH POMEROY

My flat was inside an old, converted cottage, a Victorian style building with high ceilings and sash windows that stuck as you tried to open them. In the flat below lived a stout bald-headed man in his late fifties with a creepy laugh and a dodgy right eye. Often, he'd appear at his front door when I entered the building. I'm sure he watched me all the time from behind the dirty grey net curtains that hung in his window.

He shuffled around town in worn-out shoes, dressed in the same everyday brown slacks matched with a burgundy jumper. Every day he looked lost and forlorn. I crossed the street to avoid him, never wanting to be near him or to get to know him.

He was the former caretaker at my old school. Rumour had it he fiddled about with more than just the boiler, although it was never proven. I read about his death in the local paper; he died of a heart attack in front of the log fire, a glass of red wine by his side and a faded 1940s pinup photo on his lap. Only the vicar attended the caretaker's funeral. His unmarked grave went unloved. Over time, weeds grew where his decaying body lay, offering up a small array of colour as dandelions and buttercups bloomed.

I moved out of the area soon after as a job took me to London. Years later I returned and found the old Victorian cottage demolished to make way for flats. A friend told me that as they'd cleared out the cottage, they found the old caretaker's diaries underneath the floorboards. His name was Ron Williams, a former soldier in World War II. He fought for his country from a mere eighteen years of age and bore the scars of the deaths of all the young who served beside him and died at his feet.

Inside the diary was a buttercup, brown and paper-thin, preserved within love letters from his childhood sweetheart. Over time, the love and the letters faded, just like the gunfire.

His sweetheart fell in love with another.

His life fell apart.

I saw a buttercup today. I picked it up and as I held it, I remembered him.

# TODAY IS A GOOD DAY TO DIE
## BY FIONA JACOB

He shot at me twice but hit me once. The glass between us shattered into a million shards.

One gunshot penetrated the left side of my chest underneath the left clavicle. It felt like I was hit hard by a baseball bat. My knees buckled under the force of the bullet that pressed me backwards onto the cold tiled floor in a weird slow-motion fall. A searing pain of hot metal spread inside me like lit charcoal. A blue ceramic mug with freshly brewed coffee slipped out of my hand and shattered on the floor. My confused fingers felt a wet stickiness that spread across the brown tiles in a red tide. I felt a fog of stone-cold dread descend over me.

"Shit, this hurts like the bejesus," I said to nobody.

My ears, muffled from the loud pop-shots, heard a distant voice over the hospital tannoy, "code grey, operating room." Doctors' pagers at the reception desk shrieked in a cacophony of wretched disharmony. Rapid footsteps, distant screams, panicked faces.

My stethoscope, with its small grey and pink teddy, lay strewn in the expanding scarlet pool.

"Get out of the fucking way," Dr Rabea, the paediatric surgeon, said as he suppressed a scream. I had never heard him curse, nor had I smelled the stench of his Ramadan breath so close to my face. He tore open my tattered white doctor's coat and red silk blouse tainted by black soot, and turned his head away as he exposed my breasts. With surgical fingers, he explored the entry wound. It felt like a twisting hot knife inside my chest.

Hordes of soldiers with AK47s cocked, swarmed and formed a cordon around the bewildered shooter, who continued to scream "Kafirah." His eyes were narrowed with disgust that they would protect this infidel western nurse and not him.

Trolley wheels squeaked. I levitated into arms. Large needles. Cold fluids. I heard my distorted, gurgled breaths and the snap of metal handcuffs. In my morphine haze, I saw the shooter being dragged away on knees like a rabid dog.

Today was a good day to die after all, I thought as a 9mm calibre bullet with my DNA remained lodged in the daffodil-coloured wall.

# PART V

# UNRELIABLE NARRATOR

An Unreliable Narrator can be defined as any narrator who misleads readers, either deliberately or unwittingly. Many are unreliable through circumstances, character flaws or psychological difficulties. In some cases, a narrator withholds key information from readers, or they may deliberately lie or misdirect.

> *While the term is fairly new—it was first used by literary critic Wayne C. Booth in 1961—unreliable narrator examples date back hundreds of years. Medieval poet and chronicler Geoffrey Chaucer used various unreliable narrators in* The Canterbury Tales, *for example in the bragging and exaggerating character, the* Wife of Bath. *Some Shakespearean characters could be described as unreliable. Could we trust Hamlet, in his grief and paranoia, to tell us the whole truth and nothing but the truth?*
>
> — Jericho Writers

At this point in the program, it's a good time for the writer to reference back to their Character Template. To look at some of the things they filled out, as they might include them in this week's exercise. Did you make up that your character was a vicar, a bond trader on Wall Street, a dope farmer in the mountains of Oregon? This exercise is written in the first person, the writer themselves becomes the Unreliable Narrator.

Think about Carrie Preston's character, Elsbeth Tascioni in *The Good Wife*. She was a wacky-dressed, disorganized, coffee-dropping lawyer who you'd imagine would lose in court every time. But quite the opposite, she was a wizard in the courtroom and never lost a case. Sort of like Columbo.

In Gillian Flynn's *Gone Girl* (which was so well done it's referenced in almost every article written about the Unreliable Narrator) there were two unreliable narrators. The book is told through alternating accounts of both the husband, Nick Dunne, and through the diary entries of his wife, Amy Dunne. We are unsure which character to trust in this unfolding struggling marriage. Coupled with the fact that they both tell lies which makes them untrustworthy and unreliable. You know what I'm referring to here. That gradual sense that all is not what it seems.

> *There are three main ways to write an unreliable narrator. One is through tone and voice, another is through factual discrepancy, and another is through language itself, which is trickier to pull off.*
>
> — Jack Grapes

For the sake of the class assignment, the writer is asked to work with tone and voice, or factual discrepancies.

Just like we don't want to be thought of as a liar we, for sure, don't want to be thought of as unreliable. But we are all unreliable to some degree, just like we are all liars, to some degree. *I'm really not that bright* when you have an IQ over 150. *My writing assignment for this week sucks,* when inside you know you nailed it. Have you ever been in relationship with a "withholder"? They are so unreliable.

Sometimes it's what is not said that adds layers to an unreliable narrator. That friend you meet for supper and shares all about the joys of married life, how her husband is wonderful, caring, generous and yet there is that look in her eye. She is withholding. How can you believe anything she is sharing? Grab your template, write in first person, build her out on the page, so the reader is hooked.

# DEVOUT

## BY MARY WHITE

Every day I am torn between good and evil. Today, I stand before three tiers of votive candles. I light one and pray in silence. I need the guidance only God can give. I pray to Jesus, my lord and savior. I pray to the Virgin Mary. I pray to all the saints I can recall. I pray every day with my rosary, but don't get any answers.

As a devout Catholic, I need not worry. I go to confession to be absolved of my wrongdoings. It's the ultimate magic trick. The fires of Hell are real. I don't want to go there when I die. Heaven is a real place with a gate where God awaits, clipboard in hand, culling the faithful from the masses. Last night I dreamed I met God at the gate, and he wore reading glasses. I awakened in a panic. How could God need reading glasses? The image still haunts me!

Have faith. Faith is all that matters. Faith in miracles. Faith in the unseen. Faith in the mystery. Faith, rosaries, confession and candle lighting will keep me safe. All is as it should be under the watchful eyes of God.

In faith, I follow concrete rules based on facts that bring me comfort. God, as the Father, is male. Men are superior to women.

Since men are closer to God, women can never hold high positions in the Church. Human beings are either male or female, nothing in between. Only men and women can lie together, but not until after marriage. Thank goodness there are clear rules and delineations for hierarchy of power, gender identity and sexual conduct. At times, I am in a quandary because I don't understand why gender identity or sexual conduct matter to God or why one gender is favored over another. No one can give me a solid reason. There is also a puzzling lack of evidence that men are superior. But these facts are written in the Bible. I try not to question them, just like I didn't question the priest who put his hand under my dress in confirmation school.

Questions are inevitable. My devout faith never waivers. I just follow the rules like a lemming to the sea.

# MERCY, MERCY ME
## BY FIONA JACOB

I never had any intention of being a paramedic. I'd always wanted to be a doctor, but I coasted through high school on cigarettes, booze, and bad boyfriends. So, not quite the path to medical school.

The cool thing about my job is that I get to save lives. I am proud to be the person you rely on at the worst moments in your life.

Whether you are having a heart attack,

Whether you are slumped over the steering wheel after a collision,

Whether your baby decides to be born early in the shopping mall.

My first incursion into this world was when I was eight years old. My brother, who was ten, fell out of the leafy green sycamore in our backyard. There was a loud thump, then he slumped over like a sack of potatoes. I giggled. He howled and said he couldn't move his legs. He even passed out. The spineless wimp.

Ten minutes later an ambulance rolled up. Two paramedics with taut faces and scarlet red backpacks choreographed a tango of rescue sequences and dead-lifted him onto the steel and orange stretcher. I was transfixed.

Here's the thing, I graduated first in my class. "A gifted compassionate paramedic," the head of the ambulance service said before he handed me my epaulets and gold medal. My proud brother waved and smiled at me from his powered wheelchair in the front row.

On my first shift, Jim, my paramedic partner, blue-lighted us to a house fire. The December night air was a mix of frost and thick black acrid smoke. The semi-detached house was engulfed in red-orange flames. Two lifeless adult bodies lay on the grass, two smaller bodies alongside them.

I watched an exhausted fireman carry a small body, a little girl about four years old, out of the house. As Jim raced us back to the paediatrics hospital, Kayleigh was barely alive with 80% burns and a trachea full of soot. I stroked her singed blonde curly hair and sang *Itsy Bitsy Spider* to her as I overdosed her with morphine. She stopped breathing and dropped her pink scorched teddy bear on the ambulance floor.

I've kept her teddy bear ever since in my locked 'mercy' cupboard.

# MY LAST DAY AT THE BANK
## BY KRYSTEEN DVORACEK

I felt numb when it happened. My manager called me into the meeting room, the discreet one, near the lifts. "Ian," he said. "We've restructured your role, which means we're going to let you go." I stared at George, his pale face glistening with sweat, brown eyes downcast, reading from HR's script. Part of me felt shocked, part detached. Like I was outside my body, looking down at us. I liked George, but that didn't mean I'd make it easy. "You're sacking me, you mean," I said. "Let's call it what it is." I knew whatever I said, it wouldn't count. Just like thirty years' loyal service wouldn't count.

I loved working here. I'd joined the Bank straight out of high school, all gangly limbs. I remember starting as a junior teller, spending Friday nights down the pub with the blokes from the branch, telling jokes and downing beers. They called me Pocket Rocket because I could balance a register faster than anyone. I loved being Rocket. Way better than being boring old Ian. Here I was good at something. Here I fitted in.

The nickname Pocket Rocket stuck and so did I. I stuck around long enough to make branch manager, long enough to get promoted to head office, long enough to have three hundred people report to me and make Operations Manager Band B. Wherever the mothership sent me, I went. Whatever it asked me to do, I did. You've got to put in the work to get the pay. My ex-wife never got that. Never got that I was doing it for her and the kids. Constantly nagging at me to spend more time at home. All those mornings I'd get up grey and exhausted and haul myself into work. And she repays me by leaving.

Now the mothership dumping me as well? That's not what I signed up for. I wasn't going to go quietly. I'd be their Pocket Rocket that's for sure. I ripped the fire extinguisher off the wall, wrapped my arms around it and hurled us both through the plate glass window. Time to make those fickle fuckers pay. Go off like a Rocket.

I made sure they wouldn't forget me, or my last day at the Bank.

# HIDE AND SEEK
## BY BIANCA BAZIN

I had a happy childhood; I think. I had parents who loved me, and siblings with whom I played, ran, and hid. We were interwoven, like a tacky spider's web. Our dinner table was both stormy and silent, with various hand squeezes from underneath the table. My mother's crablike arms ensured a roof over my head and fashionable long-sleeved tops and trousers hid our scratches and bumps. Mum said I inherited her ability to fall down, like Humpty Dumpty.

When we were all together, we lived in a small brick house. My mother and I visited the hospital regularly, so its proximity was convenient, especially when I arrived with a chunk of ashtray in my wrist and a crack in my skull. "And now we know not to play with Dad's ashtrays," my mother joked on the drive home, and I giggled. The chimes on our porch clinked that night as I sang along, brewing to a clash with each step as my father thundered up the stairs, me in his study and the others in a closet, praying it would stop.

As I grew older, the exhilaration continued. We moved from place to place in a game of hide and seek. My favourite house, Kingfishers, belonged to Aunt Rebecca. It was an ivy-clad stone house with lead windows, a smoking chimney and a sloping garden leading to a forest called Abbotswood. In the garden were a row of apple trees which we picked in summer. Those we missed fell and rotted, infested with maggots by autumn. My memory is etched with the alcoholised stench of those rancid apples.

So, my childhood never failed to delight. Each time Dad found us, out we would run, like tag or it, into a forest and the game would restart. The fun is over now that mum is gone; the game went wrong when Dad brought a gun. "We were just playing hide and seek!" I begged the police. The odour of rot prickled my eyes and they started to stream. Today they both wait, mum in silence beneath the earth and the trees, and Dad like a storm behind bars that clink like the chimes on our porch.

# STEPPING OVER CHRISTMAS
## BY TRISH POMEROY

Home was a tired run-down shack out in the suburbs, untidy and uncared for. Wind howled through broken windows and icicles formed inside the bathroom. Our Christmas tree lacked fairy lights and Christmas presents. I hoped Santa would visit, but hunger came instead.

I don't care for winter, with its grey days, constant deluge of rain and winds cold enough to freeze your tits off.

I don't care to leave the house either. Too many people, all rude and miserable. No one smiles anymore. They stare at their phones as if life begins and ends at their fingertips.

If I'm honest, I don't care about anything. Not anymore.

I was born late September 1976, the result of a drunken Christmas shag. Mum drank for as long as I remember. If she wasn't yelling from the top of her lungs, she'd be crying her heart out on the sofa. She blacked out often. She couldn't remember if she had a child, a job, or a glass of wine. She prayed to God for forgiveness, prayed for another drink, but never for sobriety.

She'd hold onto the gold cross and chain she wore around her neck as if that would bring her redemption. I prayed she'd strangle herself with it.

I hated her. I was unwanted and unloved. She made my life as worthless as hers. She drank to block out her pain. I closed off my heart to block mine.

One day, she beat me black and blue with her drunken fists. I was too small to fight back, too afraid, too stupid. She pushed and pushed until I pushed back.

I pushed back hard.

I pushed her down the stairs and watched her crash on every stair. She moaned in agony as she landed at the bottom, bones broken and barely breathing.

I felt nothing as I stepped over her pathetic, messed up body. I walked out the door and left her to shrivel and die.

Outside, I breathed again. The sky was as grey as my mood, the bitter wind ripped through to my bare bones, as the deluge of rain washed away my sins.

It was Christmas eve.

I don't much care about Christmas, but that one was the best.

# AN UNEXPECTED LIFE
## BY TSILAH BURMAN

I was born in Alexandria, Egypt, a descendent of Cleopatra.

My parents joined a cult that committed mass suicide. It left me sad and orphaned at the age of five. An American couple, who lived in Cambridge, Massachusetts, adopted me. We summered on the Cape and wintered in Aspen. I felt like I never had enough.

At fifty, I am 5'6," with long slender legs chiseled from biking, swimming and marathons. My adopted father, short and plump, was a tenured professor of microbiology at Harvard University and my adopted mother was a Mama Cass type, Grammy award-winning recording artist. I am fierce like my ancestors, a tai chi master and black belt in Krav Maga. I drive fast to let off steam when life gets hot—almost every day. I had a charmed life, but always felt different; not just because of my olive-toned skin.

I feared abandonment. Since elementary school, my best friends were the trees and plants who shared their wisdom with me, as I laid out my secrets before them.

I fell in love for the first time in graduate school. He was a year older than me and was working on a Ph.D. in spiritual psychology. He was the product of two Haight-Ashbury hippies, who were locked up in a psych ward after blowing their minds on acid. We both felt deserted by parents.

Instead of being happy with my new relationship, I was consumed by a traumatic past life regression of being beheaded by the person I was now in love with. I got into my emerald corvette, put down the top and headed for the Pacific Coast Highway. My locks danced in the wind; warm rays of the sun caressed my soul.

In an instant, I was transported in a turquoise spaceship to a cloud mattress, where I was surrounded by a piercing golden light. Tendrils tickled my bare skin.

I woke up from a coma four months later, having survived a head-on crash. The gift of my survival was psychic abilities, which started my career as a futurist, plant whisperer and intuitive healer.

Life is a journey. Unexpected events took me on the path I was meant to travel.

# CEDAR-WOOD DOORS
## BY MARGO GEORGE

The hand-crafted cedar-wood door creaked open into the Moroccan Riad where I worked. The reddish-brown wood was detailed with ornate, exquisite carvings, and a large black wrought-iron latch.

Inside I prepared breakfast for guests and cleaned. At the end of my shift, I left the tranquillity of this safe haven, jumped on my scooter and sped along narrow-cobbled streets, through the hullabaloo of locals, tourists, street vendors, tuk-tuks, pony and traps, endless souks of silver, brass, wood and textiles. I greeted high spirited people, kind people, people I grew up with. I braked sharp and popped ten dirhams into the outstretched hand of the elderly lady sat on the ground next to a box of kittens.

I parked up and opened another ironclad door into my home. In the dim light, I made out the figure of my mother in a chair, dressed in black. The kitchen sink was piled high with crockery, and empty food cartons. It smelt of stale sweat and piss. Anger welled up in my gut. I picked up my mother's tumbler of Jägermeister and smashed it on the stone floor. Fear in her eyes, she cried pathetic tears. "How can you be this useless?" I said. Possessed with rage, I detested her weakness. She would not stand up to my father when he beat me senseless. She deserved her fear.

I removed my brown hijab and kaftan. My sleek black hair fell loose over my shoulders. I slipped into black stilettos and a long green silk low cut dress, adorned with pink flamingos, which revealed my slender silhouette. With a dance in my step, I headed out into the vibrant streets again.

I got to a familiar door, the same ornate style, and entered a small low-lit cafe with bright green walls. A man sat in the corner alone, smoking a shisha. He smiled at me. Three women screeched and showered me with hugs and laughter. Our chatter dominated the space as we put the world to rights.

Just before midnight I crept back through the door of my home, with the man from the cafe, with the shisha.

# THE SHOVEL
## BY CHRISTINE MANDER

It's almost dark outside. The rain is lashing down, and the wind is strong. I have to go out later and I'm not looking forward to it. I promised I'd help my neighbour with a task in the garden. He wouldn't say what it was but hey, he's helped me often enough. Heaven knows why he has to do it this late on though. The only thing he would say was that I'd need a shovel.

I must have been crazy to say I'd help him without knowing what we're doing. His wife will be furious with him. They argue all the time. Come to think of it, I don't see why she can't help him. She must be at least as strong as me. They had a real humdinger of a fight last night. Usually, I hear them shouting through the wall, but it doesn't last too long. This time it seemed to go on for hours, getting louder and louder and then suddenly nothing. They must have come to some agreement, I suppose. Either that or they were worn out from all the shouting.

I feel sorry for him. He always seems to have the worst of it and it's always her voice I hear the loudest. I have seen him with bruises and scratches on his face, but that was a while ago now. Recently it's just been a bit of shouting. When you see them out together, they look like a loved-up couple. He's always calling her darling and can't do enough for her. He treats her like a queen. She doesn't seem to realise how lucky she is. I don't think I've ever heard her say thank you and she doesn't seem to do much for him.

I don't understand people and their relationships. I'm happier being on my own, it's much less hassle. I'd better get togged up to go out. I just heard some thunder and lightning too. I'd hoped whatever it is, it would wait until tomorrow, given this awful weather. He was very clear though, it had to be done tonight. I can't let him down; he'll not find anyone else to help him at this late stage.

# THE PERFECT BABY
## BY HILDA RHODES

My baby girl stared up at me with her big blue eyes. As I rocked her pink wooden cot, I recalled this afternoon's meeting. I'd caught sight of myself in the mirror in the church hallway before going in; my short curly hair brushed back behind my ears, my face devoid of make-up, a pink fluffy cardigan and a heart-shaped necklace. Behind me the Virgin Mary's picture, draped in a blue shawl, her head bowed, she gazed down with love at baby Jesus cuddled in her arms.

The meeting was a mixed bunch of people; drugs and alcohol don't distinguish their victims. I'd shared my story. My parents had me classified as ADHD. At twelve, I'd been sexually abused by my seventeen-year-old stepbrother. Mum had yelled at me and told me I was a sinner.

At eighteen, I'd been drugged, and gang raped at a party. My parents didn't believe in abortion. They kept the baby. My Mum stole him. He called her Mum. I hated her for that. I ran away.

I'd been homeless, hooked on drugs and alcohol when the priest saw me in his church. He found an apartment for me and my baby girl, my second child. He saved us.

The priest had told me to put my baby to bed before he and his friend arrived. I looked in the full-length mirror. My firm breasts protruded over the top of the red leather corset; gold tassels dangled from my pert nipples. A chain skirt revealed my shaved pussy. My thigh-length black boots had six-inch stiletto heels. The leather whip lay on the bed next to the black mask.

My baby's big blue eyes watched me get ready as she'd sat in her high chair. She hadn't eaten her mashed banana. She hadn't cried when I lifted her from her high chair. She hadn't cried when I cuddled her like the Virgin Mary cuddled baby Jesus. She hadn't cried when I kissed her golden curls. She hadn't cried when I laid her in her pink wooden cot. I wasn't worried, I knew she was okay. Her batteries had run out. I would replace them when I changed her nappy in the morning.

# ADDENDUM BY JACK GRAPES

Actors—very few, perhaps—come to a role fully sketched out with biographical backstory, sub-text, motivations, and the beat-by-beat, moment-to-moment emotions and intentions in their transactions with the other characters in a specific scene. The actor discovers and "finds" their character through a process of rehearsals. In French, the word for a theatrical rehearsal is *repetition*. In English, the root of the word "to re-hearse" implies the plowing of a furrow in a field again and again. Whether plowing and plowing, or repeating and repeating, the concept implies that as writers, we discover our fictional character through a process of repetition, writing and writing, rewriting and rewriting, layer by layer, one degree at a time, and each time we continue our process, we discover new facts, new opinions, new ways for the fictional character to speak. It's not all mapped out at once. We build our fictional characters piece by piece.

In a film, the rehearsal process is usually minimal, but great actors learn to work quickly. In the rehearsal process of a theatrical nature, a play for instance, the actor "finds" their character bit by bit, from one rehearsal to the next, and often the actor avoids too much pre-planning, but lets the sense of the character come to them in layers and by degrees, one moment at a time.

The same process should be the writer's process as well. The writer can discover, or "find" their fictional character through the writing, not just through pre-planned notes and intellectual conceptions. My method for the writer who is creating and building a character is the same method as the actor's "finding" the character through rehearsals. They both do it by degrees, layer upon layer of lies. Part of these layers are created by degrees, increments of lies. The art of fiction lies in our ability to construct an authentic being out of a series of lies. We don't do this in one gulp. It's a process. And this process can be learned, the same way we learn techniques for dance, playing a musical instrument, or achieving mastery in a sport.

The various techniques can be applied incrementally, so that gradually we become less ourselves and more like the fictional person we are creating and building. The writer might start with a few little lies, which I call expositional or minor details that have to do with an event or an object. Our lies, being 20% of what we write, are fiction, and the other 80% is true, details and feelings that come from the writer's own life. When we get to a ratio of 50% lies and 50% true, we are hovering, as it were, on the tipping point, what Ezra Pound calls the unwobbling pivot.

Many fictional characters are split pretty evenly, 50% based on the author's own experience, 50% made up. But once we cross that line and go beyond the 50-50 balance, the point tips, the pivot wobbles. The tables have been turned. 80% of the character we have been sculpting, bit by bit, layer by layer, is no longer us at all. It's someone else, even when 20% is still rooted in who we are. The writer feels the shift. I'm Ishmael here, but over there, Ishmael is someone else, someone not me.

"Where'd that bloke come from!" the writer says, as if it just happened by accident. But it was no accident. The writer had a series of techniques that were practiced and laid out in a series of trials: the writing was going along and changing in the process. The writer is creating a character bit by bit, building and constructing a fictional being that leaps off the page and remains in the reader's mind long after they've finished reading the book. Holden Caulfield, Captain Ahab, Jane Eyre, Hamlet, Huckleberry Finn. In our imaginations, they live on forever.

The writer—like the actor—feels the shift, that someone else is inhabiting their body, details and events and memories coming from somewhere else, out of nowhere. Once we cross the line of 50%, there's another shift. The voice of the first-person narrator is no longer the voice of the author. It's now the voice of someone else, the way they talk, the way they think, the words they use and the way they use them.

We can never be 100% fictional; there's always some part of us that is not dissolvable. Something inside every one of us takes part in every other one of us.

We are, even if to a small degree, the Other. And sometimes, the Other, that fictional character, is unreliable. We've been building bit by bit: But the last bridge we have to cross, in creating and building a character, is the "unreliable narrator."

Our fictional narrators are mostly reliable. We have to assume that we can trust the narrator of a story or novel to tell us their story accurately. So, the "Unreliable Narrator" is not going to be one's fictional character all the time. It's a unique situation. There are many novels where the story is told by an "unreliable narrator." As writers, we have to know, not just how to create and build a fictional narrator, a narrator we can trust to spill the beans only to us, the reader, but in rare cases, we have to know how to create a narrator who is unreliable to boot. There are many different kinds of unreliable narrators, and as writers, we have to know how to create them and build them piece by piece, bit by bit.

I take my snake-bite kit with me whenever I backpack into the California wilderness. I don't expect to get bitten. But sometimes, in fiction, in making art, we are bitten by the unique persona of the unreliable narrator. And when that happens, we're ready. We have our little snake-bite unreliable narrator kit. Piece by piece, we're putting it together. First, with details and specific events and facts. Then we add the voice, the Sentences that are written not in the way we talk, but in the way the fictional narrator would talk. Maybe this fictional narrator has a "style" of writing, not simply as they speak, but a literary style that is unique to them. Think Proust's narrator in *Remembrance of Things Past*.

Think Faulkner's narrators who tell their story in a unique writing style. And then there is something in between writing like you talk and writing in a style. It's a blend of both, what many critics call "signature." Most of us write in one way, but when we sign our name, it's something we've practiced since 4th grade: our signature is not our everyday writing. It's our stamp. But it's still in our own handwriting. So, between writing in the voice of a narrator who writes as she speaks and the writing in a unique literary style, there's something we can call "signature," a voice/style that is recognizable, but a subtle blend of speech patterns and literary affectations: Voice—Signature—Style.

All these components and techniques are part of the process by which we create and build a fictional character. And we do it deliberately, by degrees, in layers, bit by bit. As the Sondheim song ends: "It's the only way to make a work of art."

*Jack Grapes*

# CONNECT WITH US

**Enjoyed Lies, Lies and More Lies?**
Please leave an honest review on your reading platform of choice. Doing so will help other people to find the book.

**Become a Better Writer – Connect with Jules Swales**
If you are a writer who would like to learn more about how to become a better writer (guaranteed):

Follow Jules on Instagram: www.instagram.com/julesswales/
Check out her website: www.julesswales.com
Sig up to her newsletter: www.julesswales.com/about/

**Publish Your Book – Connect with Maria Iliffe-Wood**
If you are a writer who would like support to help you finish writing or publish your book:

Follow Maria on Facebook: www.facebook.com/iliffewood
Join her writers' group: www.facebook.com/groups/riasreadersandwriters
Check out her website: www.iliffe-wood.co.uk
Sign up to Book Matters newsletter: http://eepurl.com/h0vPSr
Find her on Medium: https://medium.com/@maria_32943

**Market Your Book – Connect with JB Hollows**

If you are a writer who is wondering how to get your words out into the world:

Follow Jacqueline on Instagram: www.instagram.com/jbhollows_mamaj_author/
Check out her website: www.jbhollows.co.uk
Sign up to her newsletter: https://jbhollows.ck.page
Find her on Medium: https://medium.com/@JBHollows

# WHAT TO READ NEXT

**Jack Grapes' Method Writing Books**
*Method Writing—The First Four Concepts*
*Advanced Method Writing—The Art of Tonal Dynamics*

**Jules Swales Teaching Anthologies**
BOOK 1: *A Different Story: How Six Authors became Better Writers*
BOOK 2: *Stories from the Muses: Become a Better Writer*

**Books by Jules Swales**
*I want a Stonehenge Life*
*Declarative: 33 Statements that Changed My Life*

**Books by Maria Iliffe-Wood**
*A Caged Mind, How Spiritual Understanding Changed a Life*
*Daily Yarns, Riding the Lockdown Rollercoaster of Emotions*

**Books by JB Hollows**
*Wing of an Angel, An Exploration of Human Potential in the Back of Beyond*

**Other books published in Partnership with IW Press Ltd**
*Cosmic Collect Call: Appreciate the Mystery, Poems about Life* by Renuka O'Connell
*Leaning into Curves, Trusting the Wild Intuitive Way of Love* by Linda Sandel Pettit
*The Should Stick, Stop Being a People Pleaser* by Tracey Hartshorn

# ACKNOWLEDGEMENTS

It takes a lot to put your writing out into the world for the first time. So my first acknowledgement has to go to the nine authors who have contributed their character stories to this book.

Every one of them embraced the idea and jumped in with both feet despite any misgivings they might have had.

The meetings we had online were full of smiles and enthusiasm. I look forward to seeing how this book launches their writing careers.

Jacqueline Hollows, (JB Hollows) is such a force of nature to have on the team. I am in awe of her endless positivity, can do attitude and her capacity to keep coming up with new ideas. The authors in this book are blessed to have her supporting and cheerleading them on.

Catherine Williams of Chapter One Book Production is painstaking in making sure that every detail inside the book looks wonderful. She is so easy to work with. Thank you for your attention to detail and your patience.

Thank you to Iain Hill of 1981D, for coming up with an amazing cover design in the fastest time ever in the history of book cover design!

Michael Pastore, Zorba Editing. Every email from you is a delight to read. Your kindness and loving energy shine through. That and the fact that you do such an amazing job of proofreading makes it a delight to work with you.

I've never met Jack Grapes, but without him, or rather without his Method Writing system, this book would not exist.

And last but not least, Jules Swales is a writing teacher extraordinaire. She brings out the best in every one of her students. Her care, compassion and focussed attention to every aspect of this book, is an inspiration to me to keep doing what I do.

*Maria Iliffe-Wood*

# A NOTE ABOUT ROYALTIES

Author royalties from this book will go to support those who want to share their story of redemption so others can benefit but are in financial hardship. The royalties will help towards the cost of services required to publish a book. This could include the funding of places on IW Press programs to help the individuals to write their book, or to pay for editing services, market research, interior formatting, cover design and other costs associated with getting a book out into the world.

## ABOUT JULES SWALES

Jules Swales is a British-born poet and writer who studied Method Writing for over 18 years with her mentor Jack Grapes. She transitioned from the corporate world to teach the first online version of Method Writing with a desire to bring the power of the writing program to the world. Jules has written poetry and non-fiction, *I Want a Stonehenge Life*, *The Nanny Chronicles of Hollywood*, and *Declarative*. She has also been published in various journals and collections. Jules volunteered at Venice High School where she taught a variation of Method Writing to the students in the POPS program. She has an MA in Spiritual Psychology and works one-on-one with clients as a Creativity Coach.

Website: www.julesswales.com
www.instagram.com/julesswales/

# ABOUT OUR AUTHORS

**Bianca Bazin**
Bianca Bazin is an accomplished artist whose work spans introspective creative writing, music, and artwork. Initially emerging as a singer-songwriter through BBC Introducing, her transition to creative writing through Method Writing brought her lyrical talent to prose, resulting in narratives rich with emotional depth and vivid imagery. Her works delve into personal and universal struggles, forging a profound connection with her audience through raw, resonant writing that celebrates the human spirit's strength and the journey toward healing. Bianca Bazin stands as a compelling voice in contemporary literature and art, inviting audiences into her world of introspection and emotional depth.
Website: https://www.biancabazin.com
Facebook: http://www.facebook.com/biancabazin
Instagram: http://www.instagram.com/bianca_bazin
Medium: https://medium.com/@bazin.bianca

**Tsilah Burman**
Tsilah Burman is a writer, coach, dancer and aspiring songwriter, outside of her day job as Head of Editorial for a global real assets investment manager. Tsilah has studied Method Writing with Jules Swales for over two years. Two of her writing pieces were published in The Jade Plant Volume 8 Zine. She has a passion for personal and spiritual growth. She is working on a transformational memoir about her journey of overcoming food and weight issues and early childhood trauma to become embodied, alive and free. Tsilah lives in Los Angeles, California.

Website: www.tsilahburman.com
Facebook: https://www.facebook.com/tsilah.burman/
Instagram: https://www.instagram.com/tsilahb/
LinkedIn: https://www.linkedin.com/in/tsilah-burman-02950ab/

## Krysteen Dvoracek

Krysteen Dvoracek is currently writing her first novel, Love and Parrots, due to be published in 2025. She has won five IABC (International Association of Business Communicators) Gold Quill awards and is a former book editor (general books). For twenty years she owned and ran a successful communications agency, Transform.

Before Krysteen signed up for Method Writing with Jules Swales in 2021, she had the self-limiting belief she couldn't write fiction. Now she divides her time between writing, business mentoring, and looking after her dreamscape garden and five alpacas on the Australian bush property she shares with her husband Paul.

Website: www.krysteendvoracek.com
Instagram: https://www.instagram.com/krysteendvoracek/

## Margo George

Margo George, an accomplished Life Transformation Coach, since 2014, is based in Wiltshire in the Southwest of England. Now she proudly wears the hat of a Writer and has studied Method Writing with Jules Swales since November 2019. She grew up in Ireland and has a passion for adventure and travel. She loves to tackle new challenges both on her bike and on foot around the globe. Her mission is to shake up and disrupt how we see the world, pointing her clients towards truth and a deeper relationship with themselves, beyond the mental clutter. Margo embodies her teachings, evolving alongside her work, because staying still is just not her style.

Website: https://margogeorge.com
Facebook: https://www.facebook.com/margo.george.79
Instagram: https://www.instagram.com/margo_life_coach/
YouTube: http://www.youtube.com/@MargoGeorgeLifeCoach

### Fiona Jacob

Fiona, originally from Ireland, began her professional journey as a Nurse. Her adventurous spirit took her to ten countries as an expat, including Saudi Arabia, Kuwait, and Iraq.

After hanging up her Director's cape, Fiona worked her magic as a Master Coach and has transformed hundreds of client's lives over the last fifteen years.

In 2018, she married Wilhelm, a tall, handsome sailor, and now lives in Sweden, and speaks Swedish with an Irish lilt. They share their home with Alex, a mischievous Bernedoodle.

In 2026, Fiona plans to sail around the world; stay tuned for more of her literary and sailing misadventures!

Facebook: https://www.facebook.com/fiona.jacob4/
Instagram: https://www.instagram.com/fionafeejacob/
LinkedIn: https://www.linkedin.com/in/fionajacob/

### Christine Mander

After many years working in the software industry, Christine Mander trained as an Alexander Technique teacher. She enjoys helping people to rediscover both stillness within and ease of movement. She is fascinated by transformation of all kinds and believes in lifelong learning. This has led her to explore many spiritual and healing approaches. After years of avoiding putting pen to paper, she discovered Method Writing and continues to be surprised by the words that arrive on the page. She has found her spiritual home in the Society of Friends (Quakers) and loves the silence in Meetings.

Facebook: https://www.facebook/ChristineLAMander

## Trish Pomeroy

Trish Pomeroy loves to travel, whether it's through her work as an event manager or through creative pursuits such as art and writing. She is also a qualified Master NLP Practitioner, Transformative Life coach and Yoga Teacher.

Trish enjoys telling stories that inspire people to open their minds to explore different ways of experiencing life. This ability has influenced her career, however, enrolling on Method Writing with Jules Swales opened a door into a new world for her.

She discovered she had a talent for writing flash fiction, often with a surprising twist that delights many a reader.

Facebook: www.facebook.com/hellotrishpom/
Instagram: https://www.instagram.com/trishpom
Medium: https://medium.com/@trish_pomeroy

## Hilda Rhodes

In 2004, Hilda retired from London to a new life in Australia with her husband. The move was supposed to "fix" the "lostness" she experienced after being pushed off the corporate success ladder. It didn't. Her subsequent search has included training in several modalities, a spiritual pilgrimage to India, uncovering the impact of childhood trauma and understanding how our body's intelligence does its best to protect us. She has moved from despair to appreciating the amazing gift of life.

She started Method Writing with the intention of sharing her transformative journey.

Hilda lives in regional Victoria with her five dogs.

Facebook: www.facebook.com/hilda.rhodes.5
LinkedIn: www.linkedin.com/in/hilda-rhodes/

**Mary White**

Mary White is a Licensed Mental Health Therapist and Transformative Coach in Minneapolis, Minnesota. A creative at heart, she refers to her client work as the "Transformative Arts." Her love of writing dates back to childhood but has remained private until now. In 2022 she began to study and practice Method Writing principles which has given her the confidence and tools to call herself a writer. Other creative pursuits include piano playing, composing, cooking, dancing and beautifying her 110-year-old home. Mary currently lives with her beloved life partner Steve and Vizsla (dog) Quinn.

Facebook: https://www.facebook.com/mary.white45/
LinkedIn: https://linkedin.com/on/mary-w-269a164

# ABOUT MARIA ILIFFE-WOOD

Maria Iliffe-Wood is the publishing partner of choice for spiritual writers and method writers. She is the founder of IW Press Ltd and uses skills gained as an executive coach for over thirty years, to coach and motivate people to write their best book. Once written she works in partnership with the author to bring their book into the world.

She is the author of several books, her latest is A Caged Mind, How Spiritual Understanding Changed a Life. She always has several book projects on the go. Her next book, a small collection of poems is due to be published in early 2025.

She continues to be a student of Jules Swales.

www.iliffe-wood.co.uk
www.facebook.com/iliffewood
www.instagram.com/iliffewood/
www.linkedin.com/in/maria-iliffe-wood-52682912/

# ABOUT JB HOLLOWS

JB Hollows is the author of the inspirational, must-read memoir *Wing of an Angel*, revealing her experiences within the UK prison system and the profound impact of her non-profit work. Over the past decade, she has witnessed the transformative power of Innate Health on inmates, communities, support workers, and change-makers. Jacqueline has contributed to numerous works, including research papers, method writing anthologies, and short stories. Through her mentoring, she helps authors, creators and heart-centred leaders thrive by amplifying their visibility and impact, using the principles of Innate Health and storytelling to create meaningful, lasting change.

www.jbhollows.co.uk
www.instagram.com/jbhollows_mamaj_author/
linkedin.com/in/jacqueline-hollows-beyond-recovery/

# BIBLIOGRAPHY

Method Writing: The First Four Concepts by Jack Grapes
Advanced Method Writing by Jack Grapes
The Art of Memoir by Mary Karr
Building a Character by Konstantin Stanislavski

Milton Keynes UK
Ingram Content Group UK Ltd.
UKHW020316221124
451374UK00009B/99